Dil Se Likha Rishta

sarah shah

Published by sarah shah, 2026.

This is a work of fiction. Similarities to real people, places, or events are entirely coincidental.

DIL SE LIKHA RISHTA

First edition. May 29, 2026.

ISBN: 979-8232974763

Written by sarah shah.

Table of Contents

Prologue

Rain fell over Hyderabad like quiet judgment.

Not the loud, celebratory monsoon kind — this rain was thin, sharp, needling the streets of Banjara Hills and Old City alike, turning headlights into blurred halos and traffic signals into bleeding colors.

Inside the car, the silence was heavier than the storm.

Ruhan Khan kept both hands on the steering wheel.

Knuckles pale. Jaw tight.

The wipers dragged back and forth in restless rhythm.

Beside him, Sonia exhaled slowly and leaned her head against the window. The glass had fogged faintly from her breath.

"You shouldn't be driving," she said softly.

"I'm fine."

He wasn't.

The word fine had become his favorite lie.

The city lights smeared past them. A biryani billboard flickered above a closed restaurant, steam rising in the advertisement like a memory of warmth. Somewhere distant, an auto-rickshaw horn cried into the wet night.

"You confessed to her," Sonia said.

It wasn't a question.

"Yes."

"And?"

"She's engaged."

The word sat between them like something broken.

Sonia closed her eyes briefly. "Ruhan..."

"I know."

But he didn't know. Not really.

He knew facts. He did not know how to make his chest stop feeling like it had been hollowed out with surgical precision.

Aaliya.

The way she lowered her gaze when she spoke.

The steadiness in her voice when she corrected him.

The quiet firmness when she said, *I am promised to someone else.*

Promised.

As if she had always belonged to a future that did not include him.

The rain intensified, striking harder against the windshield.

"She didn't encourage you," Sonia continued gently. "You built this in your head."

Ruhan's grip tightened.

"I didn't build it," he said, too quickly. "It was there."

"On your side."

The wipers scraped. Back and forth. Back and forth.

He let out a slow breath, fogging the interior slightly. The faint scent of his cologne mixed with damp upholstery and the metallic hint of rain.

"I've given half my life to people," he muttered. "Schools. Clinics. Orphanages. I never asked for anything."

"And now you think Allah owes you?" Sonia's voice was calm, but firm.

He flinched slightly.

"I didn't say that."

"You didn't have to."

They stopped at a red light.

Across the intersection, a smaller car waited, headlights dimmer, engine quieter. The driver's silhouette barely visible through rain-streaked glass.

Ruhan did not notice it.

His mind was elsewhere — in a courtyard near Charminar, where Aaliya had stood correcting a child's hand position while teaching sign language.

Her fingers had moved like poetry.

"Love is not a transaction," Sonia said. "You don't donate enough goodness and get rewarded with a wife."

The light remained red.

The rain softened for a brief, eerie moment.

"She looked at me like I was a mistake," he said quietly.

"She looked at you like you were a temptation," Sonia corrected. "There's a difference."

The words pierced.

Temptation.

Yes. That was closer.

Because when she spoke to him, there had been restraint — not indifference.

And that restraint had fueled him more than rejection would have.

The traffic light turned green.

Ruhan pressed the accelerator without thinking.

The car moved forward.

Across the intersection, the other car began turning right.

Sonia shifted slightly in her seat. "You need to let this go."

"I can't."

"You can."

"I can't," he repeated — and this time there was something almost desperate in it.

The rain thickened again.

Headlights blurred.

A horn sounded somewhere — sharp, sudden, panicked.

Sonia turned her head.

"Ruhan—"

He looked up too late.

The smaller car had stalled mid-turn.

Its wheels struggled against a patch of waterlogged asphalt.

For a split second, he saw through the windshield —

A man in the driver's seat.

A woman beside him.

Her hand lifted slightly, as if bracing.

Then metal screamed.

The sound was not cinematic.

It was violent.

Ugly.

Bone-splitting.

The world folded into itself.

Impact crushed forward momentum into chaos. Glass shattered inward like frozen rain exploding. Airbags deployed with brutal force. The steering wheel slammed against his chest. The car spun half sideways before stopping with a sickening lurch.

Silence.

Then ringing.

A high, endless ringing.

Rain continued falling as if nothing had happened.

Smoke curled faintly from the hood.

Ruhan tried to inhale. His lungs resisted. Pain radiated across his ribs.

Beside him—

"Sonia?"

No answer.

He turned his head slowly.

Her body was slumped unnaturally. Blood traced down from her temple in a thin line, mixing with rainwater dripping through the cracked window.

"Sonia."

His voice broke.

Outside, the other car had crumpled inward at the driver's side.

The windshield had spiderwebbed completely.

Through fractured glass and rain distortion, he could see the man unmoving against the airbag.

And the woman.

Her head tilted at an impossible angle.

But her chest—

Was it moving?

He couldn't tell.

People began shouting.

Footsteps splashed.

Someone yanked at his car door.

He barely felt the hands pulling him out.

He stumbled onto wet asphalt, knees hitting the ground.

Rain soaked through his clothes instantly.

He looked up.

The woman in the other car was being lifted carefully onto a stretcher.

Her face was streaked with blood and rain.

But even unconscious, even pale—

He knew that face.

His breath stopped.

No.

No.

No.

Aaliya.

Her name did not leave his mouth.

It remained lodged in his throat like a curse.

"Driver's dead!" someone shouted.

Another voice: "Passenger's critical!"

The world narrowed to the stretcher.

To her hand hanging limply over the edge.

To the absence of movement in the man still inside the crushed vehicle.

Zain.

He knew that too.

He had seen him once.

He had memorized the face of the man who stood between him and what he wanted.

And now—

Sonia's body lay covered beside his car.

Zain's body remained trapped in twisted metal.

Aaliya was being rushed into an ambulance.

Rain washed the blood into the gutter.

Sirens wailed.

Flashing red and blue fractured the night.

Ruhan remained on his knees.

Water pooled around him.

His hands trembled.

Not from pain.

From realization.

He had not been speeding wildly.

He had not meant harm.

He had not seen them in time.

But none of that mattered.

Because love had made him reckless.

And recklessness had rewritten four lives.

As the ambulance doors slammed shut, he finally whispered her name.

"Aaliya..."

But the sound was swallowed by sirens.

Swallowed by rain.

Swallowed by the will of a night that had already decided its ending.

High above the city, unseen and unmoved by human intention, the sky remained dark.

And somewhere between destiny and consequence, something irreversible had been written.

Ruhan lowered his head into his shaking hands.

For the first time in his life, his wealth could not purchase undoing.

For the first time in his life, his generosity could not offset damage.

For the first time—

He understood that some losses are not punishments.

They are tests.

And some love stories are not destroyed by fate.

They are forged by it.

The rain did not stop.

Not that night.

Chapter 1

Hyderabad woke slowly.

Morning did not arrive with urgency here. It seeped in — through carved balconies in the Old City, through glass-paneled high-rises in Banjara Hills, through the narrow lanes where shopkeepers rolled up shutters with metallic groans. The first azaan of Fajr had already softened into memory, lingering like a blessing in the air.

Ruhan Khan was awake before sunrise.

He always was.

Sleep came lightly to him, like a guest that did not wish to overstay.

He stood by the tall window of his bedroom, watching the city stretch into pale gold. His house sat on a quiet elevation — white stone exterior, manicured lawn, discreet security — the kind of home that whispered wealth instead of announcing it.

Inside, everything was immaculate.

Everything except the man who lived there.

He adjusted the cuff of his crisp white kurta and exhaled slowly. The house felt too large in the mornings. Too echoing. Too aware of its emptiness.

From downstairs, he could hear faint movement in the kitchen. Staff preparing tea. Breakfast laid out. Routine.

Routine was dependable.

Routine did not leave.

By eight-thirty, his car rolled through the streets toward the Old City.

Traffic thickened near Charminar. Vendors arranged bangles in careful spirals. The scent of early-morning chai drifted from roadside stalls. Somewhere nearby, oil hissed as samosas were lowered into a wide pan.

Hyderabad was never quiet. It breathed through spice and sound.

Ruhan lowered his window slightly.

He liked to smell the city.

It reminded him that life existed beyond marble floors and silent hallways.

"Sir, we've reached," the driver said.

Ruhan nodded and stepped out.

The school building was modest but freshly painted — pale blue walls, clean courtyard, neat signage in both Urdu and English. A small banner fluttered above the entrance:

Al-Noor Institute for the Hearing Impaired — Supported by R.K. Foundation.

He disliked seeing his initials displayed so prominently.

But donors expected visibility.

He walked inside.

The corridor hummed with quiet movement — children communicating in expressive hands, quick smiles, attentive eyes. Teachers moved gently among them.

No loud chaos.

Only concentrated energy.

A warmth settled in his chest — the kind that came from usefulness.

"Assalamu alaikum, Ruhan bhai."

He turned.

Sonia approached from the opposite end of the hallway, clipboard tucked under her arm. Her dark hair was tied back loosely, expression alert as always.

"Wa alaikum assalam," he replied.

"You're early."

"I had time."

"You always have time for this place."

He offered a faint smile. "That's the point."

Sonia studied him briefly, as if measuring something beneath the surface. She had known him long enough to recognize when his calm was constructed.

"Come," she said. "There's a new teacher I want you to meet."

They stepped into a classroom at the far end.

Sunlight filtered through patterned window grills, casting delicate shadows across the floor. About twelve children sat in a semicircle, eyes focused forward.

At the center stood a woman in a simple pale green kurta.

Her dupatta was pinned neatly over her head, not rigidly — just respectfully. Her posture was straight but unassuming. One hand moved fluidly in sign, her face expressive, eyebrows lifting to emphasize tone.

The children watched her like she was light.

Ruhan slowed without meaning to.

She knelt slightly to meet a little boy's eye level, correcting his hand placement with infinite patience. When he got it right, her smile appeared — small, proud, sincere.

Not performative.

Not aware of being observed.

Real.

"And this," Sonia murmured quietly beside him, "is Aaliya."

The name settled somewhere unfamiliar inside him.

Aaliya turned at the subtle shift in air. Her gaze met his.

For a fraction of a second, she seemed uncertain — then recognition dawned. Not of him personally, but of what he represented.

The donor.

She adjusted her dupatta slightly and approached with composed steps.

"Assalamu alaikum," she said softly.

Her voice matched her face — steady, clear, without ornament.

"Wa alaikum assalam," he answered.

"This is Mr. Ruhan Khan," Sonia added. "He funds the expansion program."

Aaliya inclined her head respectfully. "JazakAllah khair for your support. The children benefit more than you know."

The words were polite.

Measured.

He searched her tone for flattery.

There was none.

Only gratitude — and dignity.

"You've been teaching long?" he asked.

"Three years," she replied. "But here only six months."

"And you prefer this school?"

Her eyes shifted briefly toward the children. They were watching curiously.

"Yes," she said. "They don't need sympathy. Only consistency."

The statement surprised him.

Most people, when speaking about charity work, emphasized sacrifice. She spoke about steadiness.

He nodded slowly. "Consistency is harder."

She met his gaze directly then — just for a breath longer than before.

"Yes," she agreed.

Something quiet passed between them.

Not spark.

Not yet.

Recognition.

Sonia cleared her throat lightly. "We're reviewing the new classroom wing plans today."

"Of course," Aaliya said, stepping back slightly. "I'll continue the lesson."

As she turned, one of the smaller girls tugged at her sleeve and signed something quickly. Aaliya laughed — a soft, unguarded sound — and signed back playfully.

Ruhan felt the sound settle into him like warmth after cold water.

He watched her longer than necessary.

Sonia noticed.

She always did.

Outside in the courtyard, paperwork was discussed. Construction timelines reviewed. Budget allocations adjusted.

Ruhan responded automatically, signing approvals with neat precision.

But his mind drifted.

Back to the classroom.

Back to the way Aaliya's hands moved — deliberate, graceful, purposeful.

He had seen beauty before.

This was different.

It was not crafted.

It was lived in.

By noon, the visit concluded.

As he prepared to leave, he found himself glancing once more toward the classroom door.

It was slightly ajar.

Inside, Aaliya distributed lunch containers to the children. Stainless steel tiffins opened one by one — steam rising, the faint aroma of turmeric and rice filling the room.

One child pushed her box toward Aaliya insistently.

Aaliya shook her head at first, then relented, accepting a small bite with theatrical gratitude that made the children beam.

Ruhan smiled before he could stop himself.

She felt... anchored.

Like someone who belonged exactly where she stood.

And for reasons he did not yet examine too closely, that steadiness unsettled him.

Back in the car, Sonia leaned back in her seat.

"Well?"

"Well what?"

She gave him a look. "You were staring."

"I was observing."

"Mm."

He glanced out the window as traffic resumed its restless flow.

"She's good at her job," he said.

"That's what you noticed?"

He did not answer immediately.

Hyderabad rolled past — fruit vendors, spice shops, a distant glimpse of Charminar's minarets cutting into bright sky.

"I noticed she doesn't perform gratitude," he said finally.

Sonia's expression softened slightly.

"No," she agreed. "She doesn't."

The driver slowed at a signal.

Street boys wove between cars selling balloons.

Life everywhere.

"So?" Sonia pressed gently.

Ruhan looked ahead.

He did not have language yet for what had shifted.

He only knew that the house waiting for him that evening would feel larger.

Quieter.

And that somewhere in the Old City, a woman in a pale green kurta would be washing chalk from her hands, unaware that she had been seen.

Not as a teacher.

Not as staff.

But as something else entirely.

He inhaled slowly.

"It's nothing," he said.

Sonia did not look convinced.

But she let it rest.

As the car merged back into the rhythm of the city, Ruhan felt something subtle begin — not loud enough to name, not reckless enough to fear.

Just a thread.

Delicate.

Persistent.

And for the first time in years, the emptiness inside his large, immaculate house did not feel permanent.

It felt challenged.

He did not yet know that destiny rarely knocks politely.

Sometimes, it watches first.

Chapter 2

By the time Aaliya stepped out of the school gates, the afternoon sun had turned honey-gold.

Hyderabad carried a different rhythm after Zuhr. The morning urgency softened into something almost indulgent. Shopkeepers leaned back in plastic chairs. Street vendors sliced guava lazily. The scent of roasted peanuts drifted through narrow lanes.

Aaliya adjusted the strap of her cloth bag on her shoulder and began the short walk toward the bus stand.

She preferred walking.

It gave her time to empty her mind before stepping back into her other world — the one waiting at home.

Her palms still held faint traces of chalk dust. She rubbed them together lightly as she walked, thinking about the new lesson plan for next week. The children were progressing well. Even little Sameer, who had struggled with sentence structure, had signed a full paragraph today without hesitation.

She smiled to herself.

"Madam!"

She turned.

A fruit vendor waved at her from across the road. "Fresh oranges! Sweet ones!"

She crossed carefully, lifting her dupatta slightly to avoid puddles left from last night's brief rain.

"How much?" she asked.

"For you, thirty."

She raised an eyebrow.

He laughed. "Fine. Twenty-five."

She selected four carefully, inspecting each for firmness. "Twenty."

"Arrey, Aaliya madam..."

"Twenty," she repeated, though her eyes were warm.

He sighed theatrically and accepted.

She thanked him and tucked the oranges into her bag.

It was a small exchange. Ordinary.

But it made her feel rooted.

By the time she reached her lane, the call for Asr prayer echoed gently through the neighborhood mosque. The sound was neither loud nor demanding. It simply existed — like breath.

Her house stood modestly between two similar structures. Cream walls slightly weathered. Green gate. Bougainvillea spilling over one side.

She pushed the gate open and stepped inside.

From the kitchen came the unmistakable scent of onions caramelizing in oil.

And cardamom.

And cloves.

"Ammi?" she called softly.

"In here!" Afsana's voice carried out, steady and familiar.

Aaliya slipped off her sandals and entered the kitchen.

Afsana stood at the stove, stirring a wide pot with measured attention. Her dupatta was draped loosely over her head, sleeves rolled slightly to avoid stains.

"You're late today," Afsana said without turning.

"There was a meeting," Aaliya replied, setting her bag down. "The foundation wants to expand the classrooms."

Afsana hummed approvingly. "Good. Those children deserve space."

Aaliya moved to the counter and began slicing coriander.

"Did you meet the donor?" Afsana asked casually.

Aaliya paused for half a second.

"Yes."

"And?"

"He seems... serious."

"That is not an answer."

Aaliya smiled faintly. "Polite. Observant."

Afsana finally turned slightly. "Young?"

"Yes."

"Married?"

"I don't know."

Afsana studied her daughter carefully. "You noticed enough to wonder."

Aaliya resumed chopping. "He funds half the programs in the Old City. It would be strange not to notice."

Afsana did not push further.

The rice soaked nearby. Meat marinated with ginger-garlic paste and ground spices rested in a steel bowl.

"Biryani?" Aaliya asked.

Afsana nodded. "Zain is coming early today."

The name softened something inside her immediately.

"He called?"

"Yes. He said he has good news."

Aaliya's lips curved without effort.

Zain rarely used dramatic language. If he said good news, it meant something real.

She washed her hands and moved to help layer the biryani — rice, meat, fried onions, mint, saffron milk — each layer pressed gently, carefully. Cooking was never rushed in their house. It was intention made edible.

"Ammi," she said quietly, "do you think life becomes easier after marriage?"

Afsana did not look up from arranging the lid. "No."

Aaliya blinked.

"It becomes different," Afsana clarified. "Easier in some ways. Harder in others."

"Harder how?"

"You share your fears," she said simply. "They no longer belong only to you."

Aaliya absorbed that in silence.

She did not fear marriage.

But she respected it.

Feared failing it.

As steam began to build inside the pot, the gate outside creaked open.

"Assalamu alaikum!" Zain's voice carried in.

Aaliya's heart reacted before her mind did.

She stepped out of the kitchen into the small living room.

Zain stood near the doorway, helmet tucked under his arm, shirt sleeves rolled, hair slightly windswept from the ride. He looked tired — but lit from within.

"Wa alaikum assalam," she replied, unable to hide her smile.

He removed his shoes quickly and entered fully.

Afsana emerged from the kitchen behind her. "You're early."

"I told you I had good news," he said, grinning.

"What happened?" Aaliya asked.

He hesitated for effect, then lifted a folded paper from his pocket. "They approved the promotion."

Aaliya gasped softly. "Zain!"

"It's not a huge raise," he added quickly. "But it's stable. Permanent contract."

Afsana's shoulders visibly relaxed. "Alhamdulillah."

Zain looked at Aaliya.

Not triumphantly.

Gratefully.

"We can start looking properly now," he said.

"For what?" she asked, though she knew.

"For after the nikah."

The word settled between them — sacred and steady.

Aaliya lowered her gaze slightly, warmth rising to her cheeks.

Afsana cleared her throat. "Wash up. Food is almost ready."

They sat together on the floor around a simple spread. The biryani lid lifted, releasing fragrant steam that filled the room instantly — saffron, tender meat, rice infused with spice.

Zain inhaled dramatically. "If promotion tastes like this, I should get promoted every month."

Aaliya laughed, serving him first.

He watched her hands as she worked — attentive, careful, always thinking of others before herself.

"You look tired," he said quietly once Afsana stepped back into the kitchen for raita.

"It was a long day."

He studied her more closely. "Something happened?"

"No," she replied quickly. "Just meetings."

"With the donor?"

She looked up sharply. "How do you know?"

"Old City talks," he said lightly. "Ruhan Khan visited today."

The name sounded different in Zain's voice.

Neutral.

Uninvested.

"Yes," she said. "He did."

"And?"

"He wants to expand the classrooms."

Zain nodded approvingly. "Good man."

She hesitated.

"Why that face?" he asked gently.

She shook her head. "Nothing."

He reached across, brushing his fingers lightly against hers — brief, appropriate, careful because Afsana was nearby.

But the contact steadied her.

"You trust me?" he asked softly.

She met his eyes fully now.

"Yes."

"Then nothing else matters."

The simplicity of that statement made her chest tighten.

Nothing else matters.

After dinner, as twilight deepened into maghrib, they prayed in the small living room — Zain slightly ahead, Aaliya behind, Afsana in her room.

Faith in their house was not loud.

It was woven.

After prayer, Zain lingered by the doorway before leaving.

"I'll come tomorrow evening," he said.

"Careful on the bike," Aaliya replied automatically.

He smiled. "Always."

As he stepped out, she watched him mount the motorcycle, helmet clicking into place.

He looked back once before starting the engine.

She lifted her hand in small farewell.

The gate closed.

The street quieted.

Inside, Aaliya gathered plates slowly.

Her life was not extravagant.

There were no marble floors.

No high gates.

No drivers waiting.

But there was something here that felt unshakable.

Security not built on money.

But on intention.

As she washed dishes beside her mother, she felt no restlessness. No longing.

Only anticipation of a future already chosen.

Outside, somewhere across the city, Ruhan Khan sat alone at a long dining table built for twelve.

His plate untouched.

His house immaculate.

His evening silent.

And though neither of them knew it yet, their lives had already brushed against each other — lightly, almost politely.

Like pages pressed together before the storm flips them both.

Chapter 3

The mornings in Aaliya's home began before the sun touched the rooftops.

Fajr azaan floated softly through the narrow lanes, slipping through slightly open windows, brushing against curtains, settling into walls that had memorized its sound over decades.

Aaliya rose at the first call.

She performed wudu quietly, the cool water clearing the remnants of sleep from her skin. The prayer mat lay already folded at the corner of her room. She spread it with habitual care, smoothing the edges as though it mattered.

It did.

Some things deserved gentleness.

When she stood to pray, the world narrowed into intention. No school. No wedding preparations. No future calculations. Just breath, recitation, surrender.

After tasleem, she remained seated for a few moments longer than usual.

Not asking for anything specific.

Just listening.

Faith, for her, was not fear-driven. It was grounding. A rhythm beneath everything else.

From the kitchen came the faint clink of steel utensils.

Ammi was awake.

By the time Aaliya entered, Afsana had already begun kneading dough.

"You should sleep more," Aaliya murmured.

"And let my daughter run the house alone?" Afsana scoffed lightly. "Never."

Aaliya smiled and began preparing chai — boiling water, crushed ginger, cardamom pods cracked beneath the flat of a knife.

The aroma filled the small kitchen quickly.

"Zain's mother called yesterday," Afsana said casually.

Aaliya glanced up. "Why didn't you tell me?"

"You were correcting notebooks. I did not want to interrupt."

"And?"

"She wants to finalize the nikah date."

Aaliya's hands stilled slightly around the spoon.

"Soon?" she asked.

"In two months."

Two months.

The number felt both immediate and distant.

She imagined leaving this house. Not forever — never that — but shifting its center. Becoming responsible for another space. Another rhythm.

"Are you afraid?" Afsana asked gently, reading her silence.

Aaliya considered.

"No," she said slowly. "Just aware."

"Of?"

"That everything will change."

Afsana nodded. "It will."

"And if I fail?"

"You won't."

"But if I do?"

Afsana stopped kneading and faced her fully.

"Marriage is not a test you pass or fail," she said firmly. "It is work. You both work. And when one weakens, the other carries."

Aaliya let that settle.

The tea boiled over slightly. She lowered the flame quickly.

Later that morning, as she prepared to leave for school, Zain called.

She stepped outside to take it, leaning lightly against the gate.

"Assalamu alaikum," he greeted.

"Wa alaikum assalam. You reached work?"

"Yes. Listen... I was thinking."

"That's dangerous," she teased softly.

He chuckled. "After nikah, maybe you shouldn't travel by bus alone."

Her brows drew together. "Why?"

"I don't like the crowding."

"I've managed for years."

"I know," he said quickly. "I just—" He hesitated. "I want to protect what is mine."

The words were not possessive.

They were careful.

She felt warmth rise in her chest.

"I am not fragile," she reminded him.

"I know that too."

"Then?"

"Then let me worry anyway."

She smiled into the phone.

"Fine," she said. "You can worry. I will continue taking the bus."

He sighed dramatically. "You are stubborn."

"So I've been told."

They lingered a few seconds longer than necessary before hanging up.

As she walked toward the bus stand, she felt steady.

Certain.

Loved in a way that did not suffocate.

At the school, the day unfolded smoothly. Lessons. Corrections. Laughter without sound but full of life.

During the lunch break, Sonia appeared at the classroom door.

"Do you have a moment?" she asked.

Aaliya nodded and stepped into the corridor.

"The foundation is hosting a small dinner this weekend," Sonia said. "Nothing extravagant. Just donors and staff. We'd like you there."

Aaliya blinked. "Me?"

"You're one of our strongest teachers."

"I don't think I belong at donor dinners."

"You belong where your work matters."

Aaliya hesitated.

She thought of Zain.

Of modesty.

Of balance.

"I will ask at home," she said.

Sonia studied her with interest. "You don't make decisions alone?"

"I prefer not to."

Sonia's expression softened. "That's not weakness, you know."

"I didn't say it was."

There was no defensiveness in her tone.

Just certainty.

Across the courtyard, Ruhan stood speaking to the principal.

He was not meant to be visiting today. But he had come anyway — claiming paperwork clarification.

In truth, he had wanted to see whether yesterday had lingered for her the way it had for him.

He saw her now in conversation with Sonia.

Her posture composed. Her expression thoughtful.

Not flirtatious.

Not impressed.

Unmoved by status.
The realization unsettled him more than admiration would have.
Most people altered slightly around him.
She did not.
He told himself that was why he kept looking.
Nothing more.
The rest of the day passed without direct interaction.
But awareness had entered the space.
Subtle.
Unspoken.
That evening, back at home, Aaliya mentioned the dinner.
Zain listened quietly.
"You should go," he said after a moment.
"Really?"
"Why not?"
"It's... wealthy people," she said awkwardly.
He smiled. "And?"
"I don't fit there."
"You fit wherever your work speaks."
The same phrasing Sonia had used.
She studied him.
"You're not uncomfortable?"
"With you attending?" He shook his head. "Why would I be?"
She shrugged lightly. "I don't know. It's his event."
"His?"
"The donor."
Zain considered this.
"Do you respect him?"
"Yes."
"Then go."
She nodded slowly.
"Will you come?" she asked.

He hesitated. "It might not be my space."

"It's not mine either."

He looked at her carefully.

"You want me there?"

"Yes."

"Then I'll come."

The simplicity of his answer eased something unnamed inside her.

That night, as she folded clothes beside her mother, rain began lightly tapping against the window.

Not heavy.

Just present.

Hyderabad rain was unpredictable — brief but intense, then gone.

She listened to it for a moment.

Somewhere across the city, in a house too large for comfort, Ruhan stood again by his window.

He had not meant to return to the school today.

He had told himself it was logistics.

But when he closed his eyes, he saw her correcting a child's hand, smiling without calculation.

He had learned to recognize desire in many forms.

This was not hunger.

It was something steadier.

Something that felt almost... inevitable.

The rain streaked down the glass.

He pressed his palm lightly against the cool surface.

"You don't even know her," he murmured to himself.

But he intended to.

In the modest house across the city, Aaliya extinguished her bedside lamp and lay down.

Her last thought before sleep was not of donors or dinners.

It was of saffron steam rising from biryani.

Of Zain's quiet smile.

Of a future already shaped in her heart.

Outside, rain continued briefly — tapping rooftops, soaking roads, making the asphalt slick in ways no one noticed.

Not yet.

Chapter 4

The dinner was held in one of Ruhan's smaller properties.

Smaller, in his world, still meant chandeliers and polished marble floors. Still meant uniformed staff and carefully arranged centerpieces of white lilies. Still meant security at the gate and valet parking along the curved driveway.

Aaliya stood just inside the entrance, her fingers lightly gripping the edge of her dupatta.

She had chosen a simple navy blue outfit — embroidered lightly at the sleeves, elegant but not attention-seeking. Her hair was neatly braided beneath her scarf. No heavy jewelry. Just small silver studs and a thin bracelet.

Beside her, Zain adjusted his collar.

"You look nervous," he murmured.

"I am," she admitted quietly.

"Why?"

She scanned the room discreetly. Conversations flowed easily among guests accustomed to such settings. Laughter carried lightly. Waiters moved like quiet shadows with trays of drinks.

"It feels... expensive," she said.

Zain suppressed a smile. "It probably is."

She nudged him gently.

He leaned closer. "Stay beside me."

"I wasn't planning to run away."

"Good."

Across the room, Ruhan spotted them the moment they entered.

The sight struck him harder than he had prepared for.

She looked different outside the classroom.

Still modest.

Still composed.

But softened by evening light and uncertainty.

And the man beside her.

He watched the way she leaned slightly toward him — not dependent, not submissive — simply familiar. The way his hand hovered protectively at the small of her back without touching.

Ruhan's jaw tightened before he consciously relaxed it.

Sonia appeared at his side.

"They came," she said quietly.

"Yes."

"And?"

He did not answer.

Instead, he crossed the room.

"Aaliya," he greeted.

She turned.

For a fraction of a second, surprise flickered across her face — then steadiness returned.

"Assalamu alaikum," she said.

"Wa alaikum assalam."

Her eyes shifted to include Zain. "This is Zain."

Ruhan extended his hand.

Zain accepted it without hesitation.

"Thank you for supporting the school," Zain said sincerely.

"It's an honor," Ruhan replied.

The word tasted complicated.

"I hope the environment isn't too overwhelming," he added, directing the comment to Aaliya.

"It's... beautiful," she said honestly. "But not overwhelming."

He noticed she did not compliment him.

Only the space.

"You both must try the chai later," he said. "It's from an old Irani café near Abids. They cater for me."

Zain's eyes brightened. "Irani chai?"

"Yes."

"Then we're staying."

The ease between them — between Aaliya and Zain — felt unforced. Natural. Like breath.

Ruhan felt himself observing more than participating.

Dinner was served in courses. Conversations shifted between educational initiatives and business expansions.

Aaliya listened more than she spoke. When addressed, she answered clearly — never shrinking, never boasting.

At one point, a guest asked her, "Is it difficult working with disabled children?"

She responded without hesitation.

"They are not difficult," she said calmly. "The world's impatience is."

The table fell briefly quiet.

Ruhan felt something like pride.

She did not need wealth to command a room.

After the meal, guests dispersed toward the terrace where soft string lights glowed against the night sky. A faint breeze carried the scent of rain-damp earth, though the storm had passed earlier.

Aaliya stood near the railing, cup of chai warming her hands.

Zain had stepped away briefly to take a phone call from work.

For the first time that evening, she stood alone.

"You handled that question well," Ruhan said as he approached.

She glanced at him. "It wasn't a difficult answer."

"Most people would have softened it."

"I don't believe in softening truth."

He studied her profile under the lights.

"You're very certain."

She took a slow sip of chai before replying.

"Certainty is easier when your intentions are clear."

"And yours are?"

"To teach. To build a stable home. To serve where I can."

The simplicity of her list unsettled him.

No ambition for status.

No hunger for expansion.

Just stability.

"And after marriage?" he asked carefully.

She turned to face him fully now.

"Especially after marriage."

The air shifted slightly.

Not dramatic.

But real.

"You speak of it like it's already decided," he said.

"It is."

He nodded slowly.

"I admire that."

"You shouldn't," she replied gently.

"Why not?"

"Because admiration can be misplaced."

Her gaze held his steadily.

Not flirtatious.

Not inviting.

Warning.

He felt it.

And for the first time, he recognized the boundary she carried around herself — not defensive, but sacred.

"I don't intend disrespect," he said quietly.

"I know."

That answer startled him.

"You do?"

"Yes."

"Then why the caution?"

She exhaled softly, looking back toward the city lights.

"Because sometimes intention and effect are not the same."

The words lingered between them.

He wanted to ask more.

To press.

To understand what she saw in him that required caution.

But Zain returned then, slipping easily back into her space.

"Everything alright?" he asked lightly.

"Yes," she replied.

Ruhan stepped back instinctively.

"We were discussing the school," he said.

"Ah," Zain nodded. "She talks about it more than she talks about me."

"That's not true," Aaliya said immediately, almost flustered.

Zain laughed. "I'm joking."

Ruhan watched them exchange that glance — intimate, effortless.

Something inside him shifted from curiosity to awareness.

This was not a woman waiting for rescue.

This was a woman already rooted.

Later, as guests began leaving, Aaliya approached him once more.

"Thank you for inviting us," she said politely.

"I'm glad you came."

"So am I."

Zain shook his hand again. "Good night."

"Drive safely," Ruhan replied.

He watched them walk toward the driveway together.

Not rushing.

Not arguing.

Simply aligned.

The gate closed behind their car.

The terrace grew quieter.

Sonia joined him again.

"You see it now?" she asked.

"Yes."

"And?"

He did not answer immediately.

Below, the city pulsed with ordinary life — headlights threading through dark roads, distant honking, faint echoes of laughter from unseen balconies.

"She's steady," he said finally.

"Yes."

"And he loves her."

"Yes."

The admission settled heavily.

He inhaled deeply.

"Then why does it feel like something has already begun?" he murmured.

Sonia's voice softened.

"Because sometimes feelings don't ask permission."

The wind shifted.

A faint chill passed through the warm Hyderabad night.

Ruhan remained standing long after everyone left.

The string lights flickered gently above him.

For the first time, admiration had crossed into something more dangerous.

Not yet desire.

Not yet obsession.

But longing.

And longing, when ignored, does not disappear.

It roots itself.

Chapter 5

Rain returned to Hyderabad three nights later.

Not violent. Not furious. Just steady — a curtain drawn gently across the city.

The streets near Charminar glistened under yellow streetlights. Water collected in shallow dips along the road. Rickshaw drivers pulled plastic sheets over their seats. The air smelled of wet stone, frying chilies, and cardamom tea.

Inside the school courtyard, a temporary canopy had been arranged for a small community fundraiser. Nothing extravagant — just donors, teachers, parents. Long tables lined with stainless steel serving dishes. Warm lights strung overhead.

Ruhan stood beneath the canopy, watching volunteers adjust trays of steaming biryani.

He had insisted on catering from an old family-run kitchen in the Old City — not a luxury hotel, not a branded chain. Authentic. Fragrant. Humble.

He told himself it was for the parents.

He knew it was not.

Rain tapped gently against the canvas roof.

"You're restless," Sonia observed, appearing beside him with a clipboard.

"I'm fine."

"You've said that three times tonight."

He exhaled quietly. "I just want this to go smoothly."

Sonia followed his gaze.

Aaliya had just entered through the side gate, holding her dupatta carefully against the rain. Zain walked beside her, one hand hovering protectively near her elbow as they stepped around a puddle.

They looked unbothered by the weather.

Almost amused by it.

Aaliya's laughter — soft, unguarded — carried briefly when Zain nearly slipped.

Ruhan felt something tighten low in his chest.

Not anger.

Something worse.

Recognition.

He moved forward to greet arriving guests.

When he reached them, Aaliya was brushing raindrops from her sleeve.

"You chose dramatic weather," she said lightly.

"I didn't," he replied. "But Hyderabad rarely asks for permission."

Zain grinned. "At least there's biryani."

"There's always biryani," Ruhan said.

The scent of it filled the courtyard now — basmati rice infused with saffron, tender meat layered with fried onions, mint, slow-cooked spices that clung to the air.

Aaliya inhaled deeply without realizing.

"It smells like home," she murmured.

The words struck him unexpectedly.

"What does home smell like?" he asked before he could stop himself.

She seemed to consider.

"Cardamom. Fried onions. Clean laundry drying in the sun. Sometimes rain."

Zain looked at her with quiet affection. "And burnt toast," he added.

"I burned it once," she protested.

"Twice."

She shook her head, smiling.

Ruhan watched them exchange that ease again.

He felt outside of it.

But drawn toward it.

Dinner began with small speeches — the principal thanking donors, Ruhan offering brief remarks about expansion plans and community support. His voice was steady. Controlled.

But his eyes kept finding her.

She sat among parents, listening attentively, nodding at familiar faces, occasionally leaning toward Zain to whisper something.

He wondered what she would whisper to him if circumstances were different.

The thought came uninvited.

And stayed.

When the speeches ended, people lined up for food. Rain softened to a fine mist.

Aaliya stood beneath a string of lights that glowed warm against the damp night. A volunteer handed her a plate.

She balanced it carefully and turned — nearly colliding with Ruhan.

"I'm sorry," she said quickly.

"No harm done."

A drop of rain clung to the edge of her lashes. Without thinking, she brushed it away.

"Have you eaten?" she asked politely.

"Not yet."

"You should."

He glanced at her plate instead. "You haven't started."

"I was waiting for Zain."

As if summoned, Zain appeared carrying two cups of water.

"Your raita," he said triumphantly, setting it beside her plate.

She laughed softly. "Thank you."

They moved toward one of the standing tables.

Ruhan remained near them longer than necessary.

"How is the new lesson plan?" he asked her.

"It's improving," she said. "Sameer signed a full paragraph yesterday."

"That's progress."

"It is."

Rain tapped rhythmically overhead.

"And you?" she asked after a moment. "Do you ever rest?"

The question caught him off guard.

"Rest?"

"Yes. You fund half the city."

He smiled faintly. "Not half."

"It feels like half."

He considered the question honestly.

"Work keeps things... structured."

"That wasn't what I asked."

He met her gaze.

There it was again — that clarity.

"I rest," he said eventually.

"When?"

"Late."

She nodded slowly.

Zain glanced between them, unaware of any undercurrent.

"You should visit our home sometime," he said suddenly. "Ammi makes better biryani than this."

Aaliya looked mildly scandalized. "Zain!"

"I'm serious," he insisted. "You support her school. It's only fair."

Ruhan felt something shift sharply.

An invitation.

Into her world.

He hesitated only a fraction of a second.

"I'd like that," he said.

Aaliya's eyes flickered — not fear, not discomfort — but something alert.

"Of course," she said politely.

Rain intensified briefly, drumming louder against the canopy.

Some parents began gathering their children, shielding them from the weather.

The courtyard thinned.

Aaliya finished her meal slowly, savoring each bite.

"You really chose well," she told him. "This tastes like Eid."

The compliment felt disproportionate to the act.

But it warmed him more than it should have.

As the event wound down, thunder rumbled faintly in the distance.

Zain checked his phone.

"We should leave before it gets worse," he said.

Aaliya nodded.

They said their goodbyes.

This time, when she turned to Ruhan, her expression held something more measured.

"Thank you," she said quietly.

"For what?"

"For remembering the school."

There was meaning beneath it.

He understood.

He was funding infrastructure.

But she was protecting sanctity.

And she needed him to respect that difference.

When they left, rain blurred the view of their departing motorcycle.

Ruhan stood beneath the dimming lights long after the courtyard emptied.

Water dripped steadily from the canopy edges.

Sonia approached again.

"You're crossing into dangerous territory," she said softly.

"I haven't done anything."

"Not yet."

He inhaled slowly.

"She invited me to her home."

"No," Sonia corrected gently. "He did."

The distinction stung.

"She doesn't encourage you," Sonia continued. "But she doesn't disrespect you either. That's a narrow space."

"I know."

"Do you?"

Rain soaked through the edge of his sleeve. He did not move.

"I've never wanted something I shouldn't," he said quietly.

Sonia's voice softened.

"Then maybe this is your test."

The word lingered.

Test.

Above them, lightning flashed briefly, illuminating the empty courtyard in stark white before plunging it back into gold and shadow.

Ruhan finally stepped into the rain.

Not running.

Not hiding.

Just walking slowly toward his car.

The scent of biryani still clung to the air.

Warm.

Familiar.

Almost intimate.
And for the first time, longing did not feel abstract.
It felt personal.

Chapter 6

The visit was set for Thursday evening.

Aaliya spent more time than necessary sweeping the small front courtyard.

It did not need sweeping.

She knew that.

But her hands preferred movement over thought.

Inside, Afsana arranged steel tumblers on a tray. "He is only coming for tea," she reminded gently.

"I know."

"You're behaving as though a minister is visiting."

Aaliya paused, leaning the broom against the wall.

"It's polite to prepare properly."

Afsana studied her daughter carefully.

"Is that all?"

Aaliya met her gaze evenly.

"Yes."

It was not a lie.

But it was not the full truth either.

She did not feel excitement.

She did not feel anticipation.

But she felt something unsettled — like when wind shifts before rain.

Not visible yet.

But sensed.

Zain arrived shortly before Maghrib, carrying a box of sweets from a local bakery.

"For hospitality," he said cheerfully.

"You're the host too?" she asked.

"Of course. He's my guest."

The simplicity of that statement steadied her more than anything else.

Yes.

Their guest.

Not hers.

After prayer, the sound of a car stopping outside drew their attention.

Through the curtain, she saw it — sleek, understated, expensive without being loud.

Too large for their narrow lane.

Children from nearby houses paused their cricket game to stare.

Zain stepped forward first, opening the gate before Ruhan could knock.

"Assalamu alaikum," Zain greeted warmly.

"Wa alaikum assalam."

Ruhan removed his shoes at the entrance without being told.

That detail did not go unnoticed.

Inside, the house felt smaller than usual.

Or perhaps it felt more exposed.

Afsana welcomed him with composed dignity. "Please sit."

The living room held only what was necessary — a worn but clean sofa set, lace curtains, a small bookshelf with religious texts and school materials stacked together.

No chandeliers.

No marble.

No illusion.

Aaliya entered with the tea tray.

For a fraction of a second, their eyes met.

His gaze did not roam.

It did not appraise.

It rested.

That unsettled her more than admiration would have.

She placed the cups down carefully.

"I hope you don't mind simple tea," she said.

"I prefer it," he replied.

Zain laughed. "Careful. If you praise it too much, Ammi will start charging."

The conversation began easily — school updates, construction plans, neighborhood concerns.

Ruhan listened more than he spoke.

And when he spoke, it was measured.

Respectful.

He asked Afsana about her health.

He asked Zain about his promotion.

He asked Aaliya about her students — not about herself.

And yet.

There was something in the way his attention lingered half a second longer when she spoke.

Something in the way silence shifted when she rose to refill cups.

She noticed.

She did not acknowledge it.

After tea, Zain insisted he stay for dinner.

"It's nothing special," he said. "Just leftover biryani from yesterday."

Ruhan almost smiled.

"I've learned that 'nothing special' here means something extraordinary."

Aaliya looked down quickly to hide her reaction.

Dinner was served on the floor, plates balanced comfortably.

Ruhan ate without hesitation, without delicate picking.

He praised the spices.

Asked for more raita.

Complimented the balance of flavors in a way that felt genuine, not rehearsed.

Zain beamed at the approval.

Aaliya watched carefully.

Not suspicious.

Just attentive.

When dishes were cleared, rain began unexpectedly outside — sudden and heavy, drumming against the tin awning near the kitchen window.

Zain glanced toward the door. "You may need to wait it out."

"I don't mind," Ruhan said.

Thunder rolled faintly.

The lights flickered once.

Then steadied.

The room grew quieter as rain thickened.

Zain stepped outside briefly to secure the bike cover.

Afsana moved into the kitchen to check something on the stove.

And suddenly, Aaliya and Ruhan stood alone in the living room.

Not by design.

But by accident.

The rain filled the silence between them.

She remained standing.

He did not sit back down.

"You've built something beautiful here," he said quietly.

"It's small."

"It's steady."

She met his gaze carefully.

"Yes."

He hesitated.

"Asking this may be inappropriate."

"Then don't."

The reply was immediate.

Firm.

He inhaled slowly.

"I don't intend disrespect."

"I know."

"Then why do you look prepared to defend something?"

Her fingers tightened slightly around the edge of her dupatta.

"Because sometimes," she said evenly, "attention carries weight."

The rain grew louder.

He understood.

"You think my attention is misplaced."

She did not soften her tone.

"I think it must be careful."

He held her gaze.

"And if it is?"

She did not look away.

"Then it must remain appropriate."

The word landed clearly.

Appropriate.

A line drawn without accusation.

Without drama.

Just truth.

Zain's footsteps returned moments later, shaking water from his sleeves.

"Flood outside," he joked.

The air shifted instantly.

The tension dissolved into ordinary conversation again.

But something had changed.

Ruhan stayed only until the rain eased.

At the gate, Zain clasped his shoulder warmly.

"Come again," he said.

Aaliya stood slightly behind, hands folded.

"Drive safely," she added.

He nodded.

The car pulled away slowly through the wet lane.

Inside, Afsana watched her daughter carefully.

"You handled that well," she said quietly once the gate closed.

Aaliya did not pretend ignorance.

"I did nothing."

"You did exactly enough."

Later that night, lying in bed, Aaliya replayed the conversation in her mind.

Not with guilt.

Not with temptation.

But with clarity.

He was not a bad man.

That was the difficulty.

If he had been arrogant, careless, intrusive — she could have dismissed him easily.

But he was controlled.

Measured.

Intentional.

And that required vigilance.

Across the city, Ruhan stood again by his window.

Rain traced uneven paths down the glass.

Her words echoed.

Attention carries weight.

Appropriate.

He had not meant to cross anything.

And yet he knew — instinctively — that his thoughts had already stepped beyond where his actions had.

He pressed his palm against the cool windowpane.

"This ends," he told himself quietly.

But even as he said it, he knew something had begun that would not dissolve simply because he wished it to.

In the narrow lane beneath steady rain, the world slept unaware.

But the line had been drawn.

And lines, once visible, are impossible to ignore.

Chapter 7

Ruhan stopped visiting the school for three days.

He told himself it was intentional.

Necessary.

Disciplined.

He signed documents from his office instead. Approved budgets remotely. Redirected staff to handle inspections.

He would not create proximity where it did not belong.

But restraint, he learned quickly, is loud.

The absence of something can echo louder than its presence.

By the fourth morning, he found himself driving toward the Old City again.

No announcement. No scheduled meeting.

Just... passing by.

That was the excuse he offered himself.

The school courtyard buzzed with ordinary life when he entered. Children crossing between rooms. Teachers adjusting lesson boards.

He felt eyes turn.

Respectful.

Curious.

He searched without appearing to search.

She was near the far corridor, kneeling beside a child who struggled with signing symmetry. Her expression patient. Focused.

Unaware of him.

He stood still longer than necessary.

Sonia appeared at his side, silent as always.

"You lasted three days," she said calmly.

"I had work."

"You always have work."

He exhaled slowly. "I'm here about the budget revisions."

"Of course."

They walked toward the office.

But Sonia did not drop it.

"You're being watched," she added quietly.

"By whom?"

"By yourself."

He shot her a look.

She didn't flinch.

"You think this is harmless," she continued. "You think because you haven't said anything inappropriate, you're still clean."

"I haven't done anything wrong."

"Not externally."

The word lodged uncomfortably.

They stopped outside the office door.

Sonia turned to face him fully.

"Let me ask you something honestly," she said. "If she were unmarried, would you be standing here pretending this is administrative?"

The question hit precisely.

He did not answer.

"That's what I thought," she said gently.

"It's not that simple."

"It is."

"No," he said sharply, then lowered his voice. "It's not."

She watched him carefully.

"She chose her life," Sonia said. "You're circling it."

"I'm not circling."

"You're orbiting."

The word stung.

He ran a hand through his hair.

"I respect her."

"I know."

"I respect him."

"I know."

"Then what exactly is the crime?"

Sonia's voice softened.

"Wanting what isn't yours."

He looked away.

The corridor beyond them filled briefly with children shifting between classes.

One of the younger boys ran toward Aaliya, tugging her sleeve excitedly.

She laughed and signed something exaggeratedly dramatic, making the boy grin wide.

Ruhan felt it again.

That quiet pull.

Sonia followed his gaze.

"She doesn't belong in your imagination," she said.

He swallowed.

"You think I'm imagining?"

"I think you're rewriting."

The accusation lingered.

He forced himself to step into the office, ending the conversation.

But her words followed.

The rest of the visit passed in functional silence. Budgets reviewed. Expansion timelines confirmed.

Aaliya entered briefly to drop off attendance records.

She greeted him politely.

Nothing more.

No softness beyond courtesy.

No invitation.

No hidden warmth.

If anything, there was a careful distance now.

He noticed it immediately.

It unsettled him more than closeness would have.

After she left, he stared at the open doorway longer than necessary.

Sonia gathered her papers.

"She feels it," she said.

He didn't pretend ignorance.

"She shouldn't have to."

The statement cut deeper than accusation.

Later that evening, Ruhan drove aimlessly through the city.

Traffic thick near Abids. Vendors closing shop. The sky bruised with approaching rain again.

He passed an Irani café and, without planning to, stopped.

Inside, old ceiling fans rotated lazily. The air thick with chai and sugar.

He ordered tea he did not need.

Sat alone at a corner table.

He tried to dissect the feeling.

It was not lust.

It was not conquest.

It was not even rebellion.

It was longing.

But longing, he was beginning to understand, can be selfish even when it is quiet.

He imagined her life — small house, steady routines, modest meals, shared prayer.

He imagined himself inside that world.

And the image did not feel absurd.

It felt possible.

That frightened him.

Because possible meant he had begun believing in something that required disruption.

Outside, rain began again — heavier this time.

Water streaked down the café windows.

He thought of her words.

Attention carries weight.

He had always believed he was disciplined.

Controlled.

Better than impulse.

But discipline is tested not when temptation is loud.

It is tested when temptation is gentle.

Across the city, Aaliya folded laundry beside her mother.

"You were quieter today," Afsana observed.

"Was I?"

"Yes."

Aaliya hesitated.

"He visited again."

Afsana's hands paused briefly.

"And?"

"Nothing."

"That is not an answer."

She exhaled slowly.

"He looks at me like he is solving something."

Afsana waited.

"And I do not want to be a puzzle."

The statement was not angry.

Just tired.

"Does he speak improperly?" Afsana asked.

"No."

"Does he behave improperly?"

"No."

"Then what troubles you?"

Aaliya considered carefully.

"He feels... persistent."

Afsana studied her daughter.

"And you?"

"I am not uncertain," she said immediately.

That much was true.

There was no wavering in her heart regarding Zain.

But clarity does not erase discomfort.

Later that night, thunder rolled louder than before.

Rain struck rooftops heavily.

Ruhan stood at his window again, watching lightning fracture the sky.

Sonia's voice echoed.

If she were unmarried.

He closed his eyes briefly.

"If she were unmarried," he murmured to himself, "I would have asked."

The truth of it settled heavy and undeniable.

And because she was not —

He should have stepped back.

Instead, he remained exactly where he was.

Not advancing.

Not retreating.

Just waiting.

And sometimes, waiting is its own form of trespass.

The rain did not stop for hours.

Chapter 8

Hyderabad's monsoon had softened by evening, leaving only puddles and a lingering scent of wet earth.

Ruhan had asked Sonia to step aside. Not for secrecy, but for honesty. She understood without question, retreating to the car with a quiet warning look that stayed with him.

He walked toward the small courtyard where the school's string lights glimmered faintly, casting delicate shadows across the damp stone floor.

Aaliya was there, gathering lesson papers into a folder, her scarf clinging slightly to her damp hair. She looked up as he approached.

"Good evening," she said softly, almost automatically.

"Good evening," he replied, his voice steadier than he felt.

The air smelled faintly of wet earth and marigolds, a strange comfort that made the words he had rehearsed a thousand times feel suddenly insufficient.

He took a slow breath.

"I need to say something," he began, carefully. "Something I should have kept to myself... but I can't."

She paused, pen hovering over the folder. "Yes?"

He hesitated. The weight of it pressed against his chest. "I... I think about you, Aaliya. Often. More than I should. I respect your life, your choices... your commitment. But I cannot deny my feelings any longer."

She froze briefly, a flicker of surprise crossing her face before composure returned. “Ruhan...” Her voice was gentle but firm. “You know I am engaged to Zain. You... should not be saying this.”

“I know,” he admitted, stepping closer but keeping a respectful distance. “I know. That is why it hurts to say it. But I had to be honest. I couldn’t pretend otherwise. Not when every moment I am near you, I feel... more than admiration.”

She closed her folder slowly, placing it on the table beside her. The string lights flickered slightly above, casting a warm glow on her face. “You are a good man,” she said quietly. “Generous. Thoughtful. Caring. But these words... they cannot be acted upon. Not by either of us. My heart... my life... is already promised.”

He nodded, swallowing a lump in his throat. “I don’t expect... anything. I just... I had to tell you. Before it became something I couldn’t control.”

She studied him for a long moment. The rain had softened to a fine mist now, and droplets clung to the nearby leaves. “You must promise me,” she said gently, “that this changes nothing. Between us, in front of others. For the sake of respect, for... everything.”

“I promise,” he said. “No action. No interference. Just... truth spoken.”

She nodded, a quiet exhalation of relief passing through her. “Then we can return to what was before. Respectful. Professional. Careful.”

“Yes,” he said, though his voice betrayed the ache beneath the control.

For a long while, they stood in silence under the soft golden glow, listening to distant thunder and the patter of the mist.

Finally, Aaliya adjusted her scarf. “I should go. Papers to grade. Students to care for.”

He bowed slightly, a gesture both humble and respectful. “Of course.”

As she walked away, he watched her disappear into the dimly lit corridor, her steps steady, her resolve intact.

Ruhan remained for a few moments longer, staring at the string lights above, feeling the weight of what he had confessed and the boundary she had so clearly drawn.

Sonia's earlier words returned: *If she were unmarried...*

She was not.

And yet, the confession had been necessary.

Even the gentlest truth, when spoken, leaves its mark.

The rain continued softly outside, tapping on leaves and stone, washing the courtyard clean — but leaving traces that would not fade.

Ruhan turned slowly toward the exit, the ache in his chest quiet but insistent.

Respectful restraint had begun its work.

But longing...

Longing had just awakened.

Chapter 9

The next morning, Hyderabad was bright but humid, the monsoon having left the city washed and shining.

Ruhan sat in his office, the steel-and-glass tower insulated from the bustling streets below. Papers, emails, and reports surrounded him, but his mind wandered elsewhere — toward a small school courtyard, damp stone, string lights, and the faint scent of wet marigolds.

He told himself discipline mattered. That distance mattered. That the confession had been necessary only to prevent the unspoken from festering into something reckless.

And yet, even as he reviewed donation allocations and budget proposals, he imagined her: the curve of her smile, the patience in her gestures, the way her eyes carried both attention and care.

He shook his head, trying to clear it.

Do not cross the line.

He had said it aloud before leaving her home.

He repeated it again now.

And still, his thoughts returned.

Sonia noticed it before anyone else.

"You're restless," she said during lunch, sliding into the seat opposite him. Her eyes were sharp, assessing, slightly amused.

"I'm fine," he replied automatically.

"You're not," she said. "You were barely present in the meeting this morning. I could have run it myself."

He exhaled slowly. "I'm thinking."

"About the foundation?" she asked carefully.

"Yes," he said. Truthful enough.

Sonia raised an eyebrow. "Then you're lying. We both know it."

He did not deny it.

"You've crossed a line," she continued softly, leaning back. "Not with her. Not externally. But in your head. Every thought, every pause, every note you take — it's her. You're orbiting her. Watching her life like it's yours to oversee."

He didn't answer immediately.

"You think you respect her boundaries," Sonia pressed. "But the truth is, you're building a world where she exists as a quiet, untouchable prize. And you refuse to see it."

His jaw tightened.

"I'm not—"

"Yes. You are," she said firmly. "Because wishing does not respect boundaries. Thinking constantly does not respect them. Admiring endlessly... does not respect them either."

Her words struck him with an uncomfortable clarity.

He stood abruptly, needing the motion to quiet the storm in his mind.

"I am doing nothing wrong," he said, quieter now, almost pleading with himself as much as her.

Sonia followed, her gaze unwavering. "Doing nothing wrong externally doesn't erase what's happening internally. You are dancing on a line you refuse to see."

He left her office without another word, walking past the glass elevators and into the terrace where the city stretched below him. The streets glimmered from last night's rain. He traced familiar lanes with his eyes, imagining small corners of her life he would never touch.

And yet he could not stop.

He thought of the string lights. Of the damp courtyard. Of the way her voice had held him accountable without ever raising its tone.

He inhaled sharply.

I will respect her life.

And then, almost against his will, he imagined how it would feel to step just a fraction closer. To speak words he should not. To notice every heartbeat, every pause, every subtle movement.

It terrified him.

Because longing rarely asks permission.

Because discipline, no matter how strong, cannot erase desire.

Across the city, Aaliya graded papers at her small desk at home. The ceiling fan rotated lazily above, carrying a faint scent of cardamom tea.

She remembered Ruhan's words from last night.

Attention carries weight.

She had dismissed them, almost effortlessly, in the morning's light. But at the edges of her mind, a small thread of awareness lingered. Not worry. Not fear. Just... vigilance.

Some boundaries, she realized, required daily tending.

Not to prevent desire. To prevent disruption.

The line existed. She would not cross it.

But she also knew that someone else's line could fray in silence.

Ruhan did not realize it yet.

But his own restraint was already trembling.

Even discipline could bend without breaking.

And he had begun to feel the pull.

The pull toward a life that was not his to claim.

Chapter 10

The following afternoon, the sky above Hyderabad was gray, heavy with clouds that threatened rain again.

Ruhan had arrived at the school, ostensibly to review the new furniture for the library. Yet the instant he stepped into the courtyard, Aaliya's eyes met his. And this time, they carried something new: controlled irritation, edged with clear authority.

"Ruhan," she said, her voice firm. "I need a word."

He inclined his head politely. "Of course."

She led him away from the children, past the classrooms where small hands painted letters on blackboards. The scent of wet earth drifted in from the open windows, mixing with ink and chalk.

"I am aware of your... attentions," she began, choosing her words carefully. "I am aware of your thoughts."

He froze slightly, caught between apology and defense.

"They are inappropriate," she continued, her eyes holding his steadily. "Even if you have not acted upon them, even if you believe restraint absolves you — they are inappropriate. And I will not tolerate them anymore."

"I... I am respectful," he said softly.

"You have been respectful in your actions," she acknowledged. "But respect is not just about what is done. It is also about what is imagined, nurtured, or pursued in secret. You must understand that some lines are not for testing."

He lowered his gaze. "I... I only wished—"

"You wish incorrectly," she interrupted gently but sharply. "You wish for a life that is not yours. You wish for me. You wish for something my heart has already given to another. That is not admiration, Ruhan. That is selfishness — even if unspoken."

Her words cut through the calm of the afternoon, sharp as the monsoon wind that rattled the classroom windows.

He swallowed, mind racing. "I did not intend harm," he said.

"Intent does not erase effect," she said firmly. "You must learn this. Immediately."

He wanted to explain. To justify. To plead. But every instinct he had to speak further met her unwavering gaze.

"You will focus on your work," she added, "and your duties to the school. And nothing beyond that. No personal thoughts of me. No distractions. Nothing. Do you understand?"

"Yes," he said quietly.

"Good."

There was no lingering warmth in her tone. No hint of gentle teasing as before. Only authority, clear and precise.

He exhaled slowly, trying to steady himself.

The anger was not venomous. It was measured, principled, and final — a line drawn so clearly that it could not be crossed, even in thought.

Aaliya turned and walked back toward the classrooms. Children glanced up, noticing the brief exchange, but not understanding.

Ruhan remained still, absorbing the weight of her words.

She had not scolded him in anger. She had not shouted. She had not humiliated him.

Yet her rebuke carried more force than any heated confrontation could.

Because it was rooted in truth.

And truth, when clear and calm, is harder to ignore than temptation.

Later, sitting alone in his car, Ruhan clenched the steering wheel lightly.

Sonia's earlier warning replayed in his mind: *You are orbiting her. You refuse to see the line.*

Now he saw it.

And yet the longing persisted.

Because desire rarely obeys reason.

Because respect does not erase feeling.

Because sometimes, knowing the line only makes the distance ache more.

The monsoon broke lightly that evening, rain streaking down the windshield as he drove away.

And the ache followed him home.

Chapter 11

The late afternoon sun filtered through the tall windows of Aaliya's small home in Hyderabad, painting the room with gold.

Zain stepped inside quietly, removing his shoes at the threshold as was custom. The faint scent of cardamom tea lingered from earlier, mingling with the aroma of lentils simmering on the stove.

Aaliya looked up from the floor, where she had been arranging freshly washed schoolbooks for Khushi's reading corner — a habit from her teaching days.

"You're early," she said, smiling softly.

He shrugged, dropping his bag near the door. "Traffic cleared up. And I missed home."

"Home is not so far," she replied, glancing toward the steaming food.

Zain moved closer, resting a hand lightly on her shoulder. "Not the same when you're not here," he said quietly.

The simplicity of the statement struck her more than any grand gesture ever could.

He knelt briefly to check the small bookshelf Khushi had started organizing — a stack of alphabet flashcards on one shelf, a row of storybooks on the next. He picked up a small card, examining it with mild amusement.

"You're keeping order here better than I ever could," he said.

"I had practice," she replied, laughing softly.

He reached over, lightly brushing her braid as he adjusted the dupatta she had tucked behind her shoulder. "You look tired," he noted.

"Just arranging books," she said.

He shook his head gently. "You always put everyone else first."

"It's my job," she murmured.

He smiled. Not indulgent, not teasing — just steady, affectionate. "It's more than your job. It's your heart."

Aaliya felt warmth bloom quietly, steadying her like the quiet rhythm of prayer before sunset.

Dinner was simple: lentils, steamed rice, and fresh chapati, with a small plate of pickles. No extravagance, no ceremony. Just home.

They ate together, Khushi seated on a small stool between them, occasionally pointing at pictures in her workbook and asking about letters.

Zain guided her gently, correcting a pronunciation here, praising her effort there. Aaliya watched, her heart swelling with quiet certainty.

After food, they moved to the small balcony, cups of warm chai in hand. The city was alive with distant honking and the faint scent of evening rain.

"You're always so patient with her," Aaliya said quietly, watching Zain tilt his head as Khushi recited a verse.

"It's easy," he said. "She's worth it."

"Worth it?" she asked, glancing at him.

"Every moment," he said simply. "Every smile, every question. Even when she frustrates me."

Aaliya laughed softly. "She rarely frustrates you."

"Perhaps not," he admitted. "But even if she did, she would still be worth it. You... you're worth it too."

Her fingers tightened around the cup. The words were soft, steady, intentional. Not dramatic. Not flashy. Just a simple acknowledgment of devotion.

And that devotion grounded her.

She realized, watching him interact with Khushi, the depth of what she had chosen. Love was not just feeling. It was action. Patience. Consistency. Faith.

Ruhan's name never came to mind. Not now.

Zain, with his quiet humor, calm hands, and tender attentiveness, reminded her of everything stable, steady, and sacred.

Later, as the evening deepened, they prayed together — a small ritual at the edge of the balcony, hands raised in gratitude. The city hummed beneath them.

And for the first time that week, Aaliya's heart was completely at peace.

Outside, rain began again, tapping softly on the roof tiles.

Zain smiled faintly, looking up. "It's gentle tonight."

"Yes," she whispered, thinking of nothing else but the warmth of home, the certainty of love, and the small, steady heartbeat of her life.

Ruhan existed elsewhere. For now, at least, he was a distant shadow, a thought that was no longer urgent.

The line she had drawn for herself was clear.

And she would keep it.

Chapter 12

The morning was calm. The sky above Hyderabad was soft, washed with gentle sunlight that filtered through the thin curtains of Aaliya's home.

The living room had been cleared to make space for the small gathering. A few close family members and trusted friends sat on floor cushions. The aroma of fresh flowers mixed with incense and cardamom tea, giving the room a sense of sacred serenity.

Zain entered first, dressed simply in a cream kurta with faint embroidery along the collar. Nothing extravagant, nothing to announce wealth or status — just a reflection of his quiet dignity.

Afsana adjusted her dupatta, her eyes moist. "Everything is in order," she said softly.

Aaliya stood near the corner, a soft white shalwar kameez pressed neatly, her hands folded in quiet composure. Her heart fluttered not with excitement, but with the weight of devotion — her promise, her faith, her choice.

The nikah began with the imam's recitation of blessings. The words felt ancient, steady, carrying the weight of generations. Every phrase resonated with reverence, grounding Aaliya in the reality of her commitment.

Zain reached for her hands gently. "Are you willing?" the imam asked.

Aaliya's voice was steady. "I am."

"Are you willing?"

Zain nodded firmly. "I am."

The exchange was simple. No flourish. No grand statements. Just intention and affirmation.

The witnesses recited the brief vows. Their words carried weight without extravagance. Aaliya felt her pulse calm as she realized the solemnity of the moment — she was choosing this life, fully, freely, with her heart and mind aligned.

After the formal recitations, Zain leaned slightly closer, his voice quiet. "This is a beginning," he said. "Not perfection. But honesty. Faith. Care. That is our home."

She nodded, absorbing the quiet assurance. "I understand."

Afsana placed her hand on Aaliya's shoulder, tears glinting in her eyes. "Your life is yours," she whispered. "And you have chosen well."

The small group shared soft congratulations, their voices gentle and warm. No champagne, no extravagance, just heartfelt wishes — prayers for love, faith, and patience.

Later, they shared a light meal of khichdi, fresh chapati, and a small serving of sweet jalebi for dessert. The simplicity of it made Aaliya feel grounded, content, and grateful.

Zain held her hand across the low dining table, squeezing gently. "Home," he said softly.

"Yes," she replied, smiling quietly. "Home."

Outside, the rain had returned, light and steady, washing the city streets. Its rhythm seemed to echo the promise of continuity, devotion, and humility.

Ruhan existed elsewhere. For now, he was nothing but a distant shadow in the clean, ordered reality of her life.

And that simplicity — the quiet devotion, the small acts of care, the unspoken faith — rooted her entirely.

In her heart, she knew: love did not need extravagance. Love needed truth. Commitment. Intention.

And she had all of that.

The monsoon clouds passed, leaving the courtyard and streets glistening in faint sunlight. The world felt orderly, sacred, and warm.

And in that small home, in a modest nikah, Aaliya's life had found its first truly steady foundation.

Chapter 13

The air in their small Hyderabad home was thick with anticipation and the faint aroma of sandalwood incense. Aaliya sat on the edge of the bed, hands clasped over her swelling belly. Zain moved quietly around the room, adjusting blankets, checking the water, and offering soft encouragements.

"You're calm," he noted gently, brushing a loose strand of hair from her forehead.

"I have no choice," she replied, trying to smile. "Besides, the children I teach prepare me for patience."

Zain chuckled softly, leaning closer. "Patience is good. But courage is better. And you have both."

The first pangs arrived as soft reminders. She gripped his hand instinctively. Zain tightened his grip, anchoring her in the world, in faith, in presence.

Hours passed in a slow, rhythmic haze — breaths, prayers, quiet murmurs of encouragement. The monsoon had softened outside, leaving the streets glistening under the city's muted evening light.

Finally, with a strong, final push, the room filled with a cry — a clear, insistent sound that pierced through every fear, every doubt, every fatigue.

"She's here," the nurse whispered softly.

Aaliya's tears came immediately. Overwhelming, uncontainable, and unashamed. She looked at Zain, who smiled gently, voice choked. "Our daughter."

The baby's tiny fingers curled instinctively around Aaliya's thumb. Warmth radiated through her entire being. Love — instinctive, primal, infinite — surged through her in a single, overwhelming wave.

Khushi. The name came naturally, chosen long ago but now carrying flesh, warmth, and life.

Zain brushed a damp lock of hair from her forehead. "She's perfect," he said softly.

"She is," Aaliya whispered, pressing her cheek to the baby's tiny head. "She's everything."

The days that followed were quiet but profound. Aaliya learned to navigate feeding, lullabies, and gentle soothing at all hours. Zain remained her constant anchor — a steady presence in the night, a soft hand on her back, a gentle voice whispering patience and reassurance.

Even the small domestic routines — folding tiny clothes, arranging Khushi's corner, counting breaths as she slept — became sacred. The home smelled of fresh laundry, soft oils, and the faint scent of cardamom from their evening tea.

At night, as the city quieted, Aaliya would sit by the window with Zain beside her, Khushi asleep in her arms.

"Do you ever think about the future?" he asked softly.

"All the time," she admitted. "But it's not frightening. Not with you."

He brushed her hair back, smiling. "It will be full of challenges. But also of laughter, of small joys, of love that grows quietly every day."

Aaliya nodded, glancing down at Khushi's peaceful face. "I can already feel it. Already know it."

Outside, the monsoon rain began again, soft and steady, tapping gently against the tin roof. Its rhythm was like a heartbeat, like a prayer, like the pulse of life itself.

Ruhan's presence, distant and unknowing, lingered only as a shadow beyond her consciousness — an echo of a life that could have been, not the life she was building now.

In the warmth of her home, in the soft weight of her daughter in her arms, Aaliya felt a profound certainty: love reshapes everything. It makes ordinary moments sacred. It turns simple meals, quiet prayers, and nightly lullabies into eternity.

And as she whispered Khushi's name in the gentle evening light, she knew this love — grounded in faith, devotion, and shared life — would hold them steady through every storm.

Chapter 14

The sun had barely risen over Hyderabad, casting a soft golden hue across the small courtyard of Aaliya's home. The smell of fresh chapati baking on the stove mingled with the faint scent of marigolds from the balcony.

Aaliya hummed quietly, arranging the breakfast tray with a practiced rhythm: small steel tumblers of chai, a plate of warm chapati, a bowl of dal, and a few slices of fresh cucumber for Khushi.

Zain stepped in, rubbing his eyes, hair still damp from the morning wash. He smiled at the simplicity of the scene.

"You've outdone yourself," he said, taking the tray from her hands.

"I just wanted breakfast to be ready before Khushi wakes," she replied softly.

The baby's coos drifted from the small bedroom, and Zain set the tray on the low table. Khushi crawled in moments later, tiny hands reaching for the warm chapati.

"Ammi!" she squealed, trying to lift the bread herself.

Aaliya laughed, guiding her little hands gently. "Slowly, my love. It's hot."

Zain watched them, a quiet warmth in his chest. "This," he said, "is all we need."

"Not wealth?" Aaliya asked, raising an eyebrow playfully.

"Not wealth," he said firmly. "Just this. Just us. Just life like this — simple, full, real."

They ate together on the floor, Khushi babbling and laughing between bites. Every now and then, Zain would lean close, whispering a word of encouragement to his daughter, or press a soft kiss to Aaliya's temple.

After breakfast, Aaliya poured herself a cup of tea and leaned against the balcony railing, watching the city wake. Vendors arranged fruit carts. Women walked briskly with shopping bags. Children ran barefoot through puddles from last night's rain.

Zain came to stand beside her, holding Khushi in his arms. "See how alive the city is," he said. "And here we are, small but enough."

Aaliya rested her head against his shoulder. "Enough is all I need."

The afternoon passed with quiet domestic rituals. Laundry folded, books read aloud, and soft duas whispered together before naps. Their home was modest — the walls not adorned with gold or photographs of travel, but with reminders of faith, love, and learning: a small shelf of Qur'an verses, Khushi's scribbled drawings, a calendar marked with prayer times.

In the evening, they shared a simple meal under dim lamplight. Lentils, rice, and leftover biryani warmed by the stove, eaten together on the floor. The taste was humble, the aroma homey, and the conversation light: plans for the garden, which vegetables to plant, and which stories to read tonight to Khushi.

Aaliya laughed as Zain fumbled with the tiny utensils, trying to balance the bowl for their daughter. She reached over, steadying it, and smiled.

"You're clumsy sometimes," she teased gently.

"Sometimes?" he said, mock offense in his tone. "I'm perfect at everything else."

Their laughter mingled, soft and steady, like the rhythm of the city outside their walls.

Later, as Khushi slept wrapped in her small blanket, Aaliya and Zain sat quietly on the balcony, sipping tea. The night air was cool, carrying faint scents of wet earth and marigolds.

Zain reached for her hand. "We may not have gold, wealth, or grandeur," he said softly. "But we are whole. Complete. And that is everything."

Aaliya squeezed his hand, eyes closing in gratitude. "Whole," she echoed. "Rich in what matters."

The city hummed softly around them, lights twinkling like stars brought down to earth. Their small home was full of laughter, warmth, prayer, and love — everything necessary for a life well-lived.

And in that humble, perfect simplicity, Aaliya understood something profound: joy is not in wealth, it is in presence; love is not in ceremony, it is in care; and home is not in size, it is in heart.

The monsoon rain returned gently at midnight, tapping the roof with soft rhythm. Outside, the world moved on, unaware. Inside, the family slept, wrapped in quiet contentment, whole and enough.

Chapter 15

The city was dark, soaked in rain, streets slick and reflective under the streetlights.

Ruhan drove alone at first, the tires hissing through puddles. He had promised himself sobriety, control, and discipline. But discipline, like patience, can be fragile when guilt gnaws from the inside.

Sonia sat beside him, quiet, her eyes fixed on the road ahead. The cafe they had left smelled faintly of chai and sugar, the residue of a brief pause that had done nothing to calm him.

"You should stop," Sonia said finally, breaking the silence. "Drive home. Sleep. Forget the thoughts for a night."

"I can't," he muttered, his voice low, strained. "I have to... I need to see it one last time."

Sonia glanced at him, her unease sharp. "You're drunk."

"I can handle it," he insisted.

She exhaled slowly, glancing away. "You're not. Not tonight."

He didn't reply. His fingers gripped the wheel tighter. The city blurred past — the neon signs, the puddles, the occasional street dog dodging traffic. He barely registered the pedestrians.

"I should have told her no," he whispered under his breath. "I should have stayed away. But I couldn't. I couldn't stop myself. And now..."

Sonia's hand briefly touched his arm, a grounding gesture. "And now?"

Ruhan's eyes were hollow. "And now... it's too late. Always too late."

The rain picked up again, hammering on the windshield, blurring the headlights of oncoming cars. The tires slid slightly on a curve, the engine growling as if protesting.

They drove on, quiet except for the occasional hiss of water and the soft thrum of the engine.

Sonia kept her warnings steady, voice calm but firm. "Ruhan, this is not the way. Pull over. Stop. Breathe."

He shook his head. "I can't. I have to..."

And in that moment, the world narrowed.

The next intersection arrived faster than his mind processed. A red light blurred through the windshield. He hit the brakes — too late.

The tires skidded on the rain-slicked asphalt. Horns blared. A sharp screech of metal tore through the night.

Time slowed.

Glass shattered. Rain mixed with sparks.

And then silence, except for the distant sound of water dripping from a cracked headlight.

Sonia's body slumped, the life that had always been careful and measured extinguished in an instant.

Ruhan's breath came ragged, chest heaving, vision blurred.

Across the street, a car lay twisted, rain streaming down its windshield. And in that other car — the lives he had no right to end — Aaliya and Zain.

Everything went still.

And the weight of guilt, immediate and infinite, pressed down, suffocating, relentless.

Ruhan's hands shook on the wheel. "No... no..." he whispered, voice raw. "Not them... not..."

He wanted to turn away. He wanted to escape. But the rain and wreckage and unbearable truth held him fast.

Somewhere, deep inside, he knew nothing would ever be the same.

Nothing.
Not the city. Not the rain. Not him.

Chapter 16

The rain fell in sheets, relentless, a steady hammer on the asphalt. Ruhan gripped the steering wheel as the tires fought for traction. Every puddle was a potential trap, every curve a hazard.

Sonia's voice beside him was calm but tense. "Slow down. Please. Just slow down."

"I can't," he muttered, teeth clenched. "I need to..."

The headlights caught something — a flash of white in the distance. A car, moving perpendicular to their path, cutting through the intersection.

Ruhan slammed the brakes.

The tires skidded. Water sprayed in arcs. The world twisted, headlights skewing into long streaks. The sound of metal scraping on metal tore through the night.

Glass exploded like crystal in the storm. Rain mixed with shattered windshield fragments and the smell of burning rubber.

Sonia screamed — a sharp, high sound that pierced his ears.

He tried to control the wheel, tried to steer them out of the inevitable. But physics and speed and water and panic refused him.

The other car hit.

The impact was immediate. Violent. Relentless.

Metal crumpled. Airbags deployed in flashes of white. The world smelled of gasoline, wet fabric, and something... metallic.

Ruhan's chest slammed against the wheel. Pain exploded across his body. The seatbelt cut into his torso like wire.

Sonia's scream cut off abruptly. Silence — thick, suffocating, and absolute — settled over him.

The rain continued outside, oblivious, hammering on the roof of twisted steel.

Through the shattered windshield, he saw fragments of life — bodies thrown, air bags puffed like ghosts, lights flickering, the city smeared in rain-streaked chaos.

His mind struggled to register. Names. Faces. Consequences.

Sonia. Alive? No. Still? He could not tell.

The other car — white. Familiar curves of the roof, the glint of rain on the hood.

Aaliya. Zain.

Something primal, urgent, tore through him. He tried the door, the seatbelt, his own limbs. Pain and rain and metal refused motion.

The world was upside down, inside out, wrong in every sense.

And then, a horrifying clarity: the other car had been them.

Sonia and... and Aaliya. Zain.

The sound of their collision — screaming metal, shattering glass — lingered in his mind like a bell that would never stop ringing.

He stumbled out of his own car, rain soaking through his clothes, heart hammering, vision blurred. Every step was a struggle, but he forced himself forward.

The scene was grotesque, unforgiving. Twisted metal, shattered lights, and the smell of wet earth mixed with gasoline.

Sonia lay still.

He did not look at her for long. He could not.

And then... he saw the other car.

Zain slumped over the wheel. Aaliya... her head tilted, eyes closed.

"No," he whispered, voice breaking. "No... no... please..."

He ran, stumbling over wet pavement, heart lodged in his throat. Rain soaked through him, merging with tears he did not realize he was shedding.

Nothing moved. No one moved. Only the rain. Only the street. Only the inevitability of what had just happened.

And then he heard it: a faint groan.

Aaliya.

She was alive. Somehow alive.

Zain... still.

Sonia... gone.

The weight of the world fell on Ruhan all at once.

The guilt, the horror, the knowledge that his choices — one reckless night, one ignored warning, one alcohol-fueled drive — had destroyed lives.

He sank to the ground, rain plastering hair to his forehead, hands trembling, voice lost to sobs.

The rain continued to fall.

The city continued to exist.

And Ruhan knew, with absolute certainty, that nothing would ever be the same again.

Chapter 17

The hospital smelled of antiseptic, rain-soaked concrete, and faintly of flowers someone had placed in a vase near the entrance.

Aaliya's eyes fluttered open, disoriented. The room was unfamiliar, sterile. Machines beeped softly around her, unfamiliar sounds that made her heart beat faster.

She tried to sit up, but a sharp ache stopped her. Confusion and fear pressed down like a heavy weight.

"Where...?" she whispered, voice hoarse.

A nurse glanced at her gently. "You're safe, madam. Just rest. You've been through a terrible accident."

Accident? The word had no meaning yet, no shape. She tried to remember—her house, the monsoon, Zain, Khushi—everything she had known felt hazy, like watercolors washed in rain.

A hand touched hers lightly. Warm. Familiar?

Ruhan.

She stared at him, confusion clouding her features. "Who... who are you?"

He froze. The weight of the world pressed on him. His throat was tight, his chest heavy with guilt. He should have explained, stopped himself, apologized. But now the words stuck in his throat like knives.

"I... I'm Ruhan," he said carefully, voice low. "I... I'm here to help you. That's all."

"Help me?" Her brow furrowed. "Help me... how?"

He swallowed, the guilt almost unbearable. “You… you were in an accident. You’re safe. That’s all you need to know for now.”

Her eyes searched his, looking for something — a familiar face, a name, a hint of memory. Nothing came.

She tried to sit upright again, wincing as pain flared through her body. “My… my home. My family…” Her voice broke.

Ruhan’s heart twisted. He could not tell her the truth — not yet. She was fragile, her mind a delicate vessel of memory and identity.

“They… they will come to you,” he said cautiously. “But for now, you must rest.”

Tears pricked her eyes. She felt a hollow ache she could not name, a missing piece in a life she thought she remembered.

In the hallway, doctors whispered in urgent tones. Ruhan stayed close, silent, watching, praying that her confusion would not deepen into despair.

Somewhere inside him, a gnawing guilt clawed relentlessly. Every choice, every reckless drive, every ignored warning — it had led to this.

Sonia… Zain…

Gone.

He had survived. She had survived. But at what cost?

Aaliya’s breaths were shallow. Her hands clutched the blanket around her. The fear, the emptiness, the sense of lost time — it all pressed down like a tide she could not fight.

“Where…?” she whispered again, almost inaudibly.

Ruhan knelt beside the bed, trying to steady his voice. “You’re safe,” he repeated. “That’s what matters.”

She closed her eyes, overwhelmed, trying to find something solid, something real. But nothing came.

The world she had known — her husband, her daughter, her home — had been erased in one cruel instant.

And she did not remember.

She did not know love, loss, or life.

She only knew fear.

And Ruhan... Ruhan knew the unbearable truth: that he was the architect of this emptiness.

Chapter 18

The sunlight filtering through the hospital blinds was harsh, cutting across Aaliya's face in wide golden bars. She blinked, trying to focus, but the shapes around her refused to settle.

A hospital bed. Machines softly beeping. A soft hum of movement. Faces she should know but didn't.

"Where...?" she whispered, voice trembling, throat raw.

Ruhan knelt beside her, careful to keep his posture neutral, hands folded loosely in front of him. He smiled faintly, though the weight of guilt pressed heavy in his chest.

"You're awake," he said softly. "You're safe. That's all that matters right now."

She frowned, panic rising. "Safe... where? What... what happened?"

He took a slow breath, choosing words as one might choose shards of glass. "You were in an accident. It was serious. But you're okay. That's what's important."

Aaliya's eyes searched the room, searching for familiarity. Faces, names, memories — nothing. Every recollection of her life felt hazy, like smoke curling in the wind. Her heart ached with an unnamed loss, a void she could not define.

"My... family..." she murmured. "Where's... Zain?"

Ruhan's chest tightened. He had rehearsed a thousand different ways to speak, and none were safe. Not yet. The truth would shatter her fragile mind.

"They... they're... gone," he said carefully, softening the words into a vague abstraction. "But you're alive. That's what matters."

She gasped, a small, stifled sound of confusion and grief. The word "gone" hit her like cold rain, leaving emptiness in its wake. Her mind scrambled for context, for faces, for meaning — nothing came.

"I... I don't remember," she whispered, voice breaking.

"You don't have to," Ruhan said gently. "We'll take care of everything. For now, just rest."

Afsana entered quietly, her face pale, eyes red-rimmed. She moved to Aaliya's side, placing a trembling hand over hers.

"Everything will be fine," she said softly, voice taut with grief she could not show. "You're safe. That's all that matters."

Aaliya looked at her mother, searching for reassurance, for a tether to reality. But all she found was gentle authority — a calm she could not understand but instinctively clung to.

The days that followed were a careful choreography. Doctors monitored her vitals. Ruhan ensured every need was met. Afsana guided her through the simplest routines: drinking tea, washing her hands, walking slowly down the corridor.

And all the while, they wove a careful story:

Sonia had been her closest friend.

Ruhan was a family friend.

Khushi — the child she could not remember — was someone she helped care for as an aunt.

Each detail was a stitch in a fragile fabric, designed to hold her together without breaking the delicate threads of her mind.

She accepted it because she had no choice. Names, faces, memories — they all floated past her, disconnected, unreal. The ache inside her chest had no anchor, no shape.

At night, she stared at the ceiling, heart pounding, whispering fragments of questions she could not name.

"Who... am I?"

Ruhan watched from the doorway, guilt etched in every line of his face. He wanted to collapse, to beg forgiveness, to scream at the unfairness of it all. But he could not.

She was alive. That was all that mattered.

And for now, the truth would remain buried.

But even buried, it had a weight.

A weight that would grow, silently, inevitably, with each passing day.

The monsoon returned softly, rain tapping against the hospital windows, each drop a reminder of everything lost, everything hidden, and everything that would demand reckoning.

Chapter 19

The morning light in the Delhi hospital was muted, filtered through heavy gray clouds that had followed the monsoon north. The sterile smell of antiseptic and faint traces of jasmine from the hallway diffuser filled the air.

Ruhan sat in a chair beside Aaliya's bed, head bowed slightly, hands clasped. Afsana stood near the window, arms folded, a thin sheet of tension outlining her frame. The room was quiet except for the soft beep of the heart monitor and the occasional shuffle of nurses outside.

Dr. Mehra, a seasoned neurologist with kind but precise eyes, leaned against the edge of the bed. His expression was measured, calm, yet heavy with urgency.

"Her brain trauma is severe," he said. "Not in a life-threatening way, but in a way that affects memory consolidation. Right now, she is fragile. Extremely fragile. Emotional stress — especially related to traumatic events — could trigger regression, seizures, or worse."

Afsana's jaw tightened. "How long will this... fragility last?"

"It's unpredictable," Dr. Mehra said. "Weeks, months... could be longer. She is capable of recovery, but the mind will reject what it cannot process. Right now, reality is a series of fragmented images. If we introduce the truth — the accident, the deaths, the identities — it could destabilize her completely."

Ruhan's hands tightened into fists, hidden beneath the edge of the chair. He wanted to speak, to confess, to kneel and cry. But he only whispered, voice tight: "So we... lie?"

Dr. Mehra's gaze softened. "Not lie in malice. Protect. Guide. The brain heals in stages. You must provide safety first, consistency, and stability. She must feel secure before memory or truth can be carefully reintroduced."

Afsana turned, her face pale, eyes wet. "But what about... morality?" she whispered. "Is it right to... to hide this from her?"

Ruhan exhaled slowly. "It's not right. But if telling her destroys her, then... then it's worse. She's alive. That's what matters. Everything else..." His voice cracked, and he bowed his head.

Dr. Mehra nodded. "Exactly. You make it safe for her first. Truth can come later. But not now."

Afsana's fingers trembled on the windowsill. "I... I understand. But my heart is screaming at me."

Ruhan's gaze lifted to hers, full of unspoken pain. "Mine too," he said quietly. "Every second. Every hour. But she must survive first. That is all that matters."

Dr. Mehra placed a reassuring hand on Aaliya's shoulder. "She will live. She will heal. But you must act as her anchor. Calm, protective, unwavering. Do not let her sense chaos, fear, or uncertainty. That is your task now."

Afsana swallowed, nodding. "I will do it," she said firmly, though her eyes glistened. "For her life. For her future."

Ruhan looked down at Aaliya, who stirred lightly, her brow furrowed in unconscious worry. Every fragment of her confusion, every whispered question, weighed on him like stone.

He swallowed hard. "We keep her safe. That is all. That is the duty Allah has given us right now."

Dr. Mehra nodded once, sharply. “Exactly. You are doing the right thing. But remember, the moment the truth is revealed — you must ensure she is ready. Until then, no risk, no disruption, no recklessness.”

Ruhan’s chest tightened. Guilt pressed from all directions, yet he nodded. Protection first. Truth... later.

And as he looked at her pale, fragile face, he realized just how unbearable the silence would be.

Because every heartbeat he spent with her, while hiding the truth, was a reminder: the line between salvation and destruction was impossibly thin.

Outside, the rain continued softly, pattering against the windows of the hospital.

And inside, a fragile life hung between memory and myth, protected by lies born of love, guilt, and duty.

Chapter 20

The small apartment in Delhi felt too quiet. Too cold. Too empty.

Afsana stood by the window, rain dripping down the glass in slow, relentless streams. Her hands trembled, gripping the sill as though she could hold the world steady. But the world had shattered.

"Why?" she whispered into the gray morning. "Why them? Why Zain? Why Sonia?"

Ruhan sat silently in the corner, his coat damp from the rain outside. He had brought her tea, tried to help her settle, but she did not see him. Could not see him. Could not forgive him — not yet.

"You..." she finally said, voice sharp and brittle. "You are the reason. You caused this."

Ruhan flinched. Not because it was untrue, but because it was everything he already knew, everything he already carried. "I..." His voice broke. "I didn't mean—"

"You didn't mean?" Afsana's eyes blazed. "You didn't mean! And yet my daughter... and my son-in-law... gone. Gone because of your selfishness!"

He bowed his head, unable to meet her gaze. The weight of the accident pressed on him from all sides. Every tear she shed, every word she spat, etched deeper into his guilt.

"I trusted you," she said, tears falling freely now. "I trusted that you were a man of honor. And now... now there is nothing but ruin."

Ruhan swallowed hard. "I will do everything," he whispered. "Everything I can, to keep her alive. To make sure she recovers. I... I will protect her."

Afsana's anger wavered, torn between fury and the desperate need to save her daughter. She paced the small living room, hands on her head. "And yet... how can I believe you? How can I let my daughter look at you and trust you?"

"She has no choice," Ruhan said quietly. "Not yet. I cannot tell her. She... she is fragile. Every step must be careful."

Afsana stopped pacing, staring at him with eyes that seemed to pierce through him. "Fragile? You mean... she is mine to protect. Not yours to hide from. Do you understand?"

"I understand," he said, voice barely above a whisper. "I know I have no right. I only... I can only serve her, protect her. That is all."

She exhaled slowly, fury softening into grim determination. "Then serve her. Protect her. And remember, if I ever find that you betray her trust... if I ever find that you place your own desires above her life... I will not forgive you."

"I understand," he repeated, nodding.

Silence fell, heavy and thick, broken only by the rain against the windows. Afsana turned away, leaning against the frame. Her grief had not lessened — it had only sharpened into focus.

Her daughter was alive. That was all that mattered.

And if keeping her alive meant enduring the presence of the man responsible, then so be it. She would endure. She would plan. She would protect.

Because nothing — not anger, not revenge, not betrayal — mattered more than her daughter's survival.

Ruhan sat quietly, feeling every heartbeat, every breath, every weight of her gaze upon him. He had been condemned, and yet he had been given a single chance: to redeem himself by keeping her safe.

And he would do it.

Even if it killed him inside.

Outside, the rain continued to fall, relentless and unforgiving, washing the city in gray.

And inside, the delicate architecture of lies and protection began to take form — fragile, necessary, and perilous.

Chapter 21

The room was quiet, filled only with the low hum of the hospital machines and the soft rustle of sheets.

Aaliya lay in bed, still fragile, her fingers tracing the thin blanket as though searching for comfort in texture. She looked at Ruhan, confusion in her wide, pale eyes.

"You... you said I was safe," she whispered, voice trembling.

"You are," Ruhan said carefully, keeping his tone soft, even, protective. "You are very safe. That's what matters."

Afsana stepped closer, placing a gentle hand over hers. "And you are not alone, beta," she said. Her voice was calm, deliberate, carrying the weight of care and authority. "We are all here for you. To help. To guide. To make sure you heal fully."

Aaliya's brows knitted. "Heal... from what?"

Ruhan exchanged a glance with Afsana, a silent acknowledgment that the moment had arrived.

"You had an accident," he said softly. "A very bad one. You... survived. But some things... some memories were affected. Your mind... it needs time to remember everything properly."

She frowned, a faint tremor in her lips. "I... I don't remember."

"That's normal," Afsana said gently. "The doctors... they say your brain is protecting you. That's why you only remember fragments. Slowly, carefully, you will regain more. But for now... for now, we need to give your mind peace."

Ruhan's throat tightened. He leaned closer, careful to avoid startling her. "And for that reason," he said quietly, "we'll help you... remember a safe version of what happened. One that will protect you from the pain."

Aaliya's eyes searched his face. "Safe version?"

"Yes," he said. "For now, it's important to know that people care for you. That you are loved. That those around you are here to support you."

Afsana nodded. "You helped care for Khushi, yes? Your... niece," she said carefully, gauging Aaliya's reaction. "You raised her, loved her, watched over her. That is what is important. You are her Ammi... in care, if not in birth."

Aaliya blinked, uncertainty clouding her expression. "I... raised her?"

"Yes," Ruhan said softly. "She looks up to you. She trusts you. And you... you have given her love, guidance, and safety."

The gentle words, the tender framing, began to settle over her. Confusion remained, but it was tempered by comfort — a sense that she belonged somewhere, that she mattered, that she could act.

Afsana pressed her hand lightly. "And Ruhan..." she said, voice firm yet gentle, "he is your friend. A family friend. Someone who has been here to help you, to guide you, to make sure you are safe."

Aaliya's gaze shifted between them, the pieces fitting — awkwardly, imperfectly, but enough. She nodded slowly. "I... I understand."

"You are doing well," Ruhan said, relief threading his voice. "And for now, that's all that matters."

Hours passed in quiet routines: soft meals, gentle walks in the hospital courtyard, whispered encouragements. Every step, every word, every glance was carefully orchestrated to preserve her fragile equilibrium.

Aaliya began to settle into the narrative. Though her memory was incomplete, the story they provided gave her a sense of structure. She could act. She could love. She could function.

And though the truth was buried, the warmth of care — gentle, protective, unwavering — allowed her to breathe, to rest, to live.

Ruhan watched her from the edge of the room, chest heavy, guilt pressing like a physical weight. Every word he had spoken, every lie crafted for her safety, tore at him. And yet, he knew it was necessary.

For now.

Outside, the Delhi rain fell softly, steady, the city washed in gray. Inside, a delicate new life — Aaliya's reconstructed world — began to take shape.

And in that fragile construct of protection and care, hope existed, even if built on silent pain and unspoken truths.

Chapter 22

The plane lifted off quietly, carrying them above the rain-soaked streets of Hyderabad.

Aaliya pressed her forehead to the window, watching the city shrink beneath her. Roofs glistened with wetness, streets mirrored the gray sky, and memories clung to every corner — the corner shop where Khushi had first toddled, the old biryani stall near Charminar, the narrow lanes where laughter had once echoed freely.

She did not remember the depth of those memories. But the pull of familiarity lingered like a faint scent, a whisper of something lost.

Ruhan sat across from her, silent. His hands rested on his knees, knuckles pale from tension. He stole glances at her occasionally, wondering if she suspected anything — if the fragments of memory would surface on the journey, unbidden.

Afsana's hands rested lightly on Khushi's small frame in the seat between them, adjusting the blanket with quiet care. She did not speak, her grief wrapped tightly in stoic control, knowing that the smallest misstep could fracture Aaliya's fragile world.

The city receded beneath the clouds, replaced gradually by the muted landscapes of northern India. Fields, distant highways, and finally, the sprawling urban edges of Delhi appeared beneath them — colder, quieter, and unfamiliar.

"This will be our home," Ruhan said softly once they had arrived, his voice carrying through the small apartment. "A new place, a safe place. No memories to haunt, no shadows to chase us. Just... us."

Aaliya nodded slowly. The words felt neutral, grounding. Safe. And for now, that was enough.

Boxes were unpacked in quiet succession. Clothes, books, and toys placed with care. Khushi explored cautiously, tiny hands brushing over surfaces, eyes wide with curiosity. Her laughter broke the lingering tension like the first rays of sunlight through clouds.

Aaliya watched her, a strange warmth rising in her chest. Though she did not remember her bond with Khushi fully, instinct told her that care, love, and tenderness were the right responses. She reached out, smoothing the child's hair, smiling softly.

"This... feels like a beginning," she said quietly, more to herself than anyone else.

Ruhan's gaze met hers briefly, and he nodded, a tight-lipped smile he did not allow to soften the guilt pressing against him. "Yes. A beginning," he agreed.

Afsana stood at the window, watching the Delhi streets below. The air smelled faintly of winter, cold and clean, with an edge of unfamiliarity that felt both isolating and protective. "We will make this work," she said softly. "For Aaliya. For Khushi. For all of us."

And though the city outside was vast and strange, inside the apartment, a new rhythm began. Meals shared on the floor, soft conversations, and the careful routines that preserved Aaliya's mind and body.

Ruhan provided, but he kept his distance emotionally — a silent penance, a constant reminder of the lives lost, the guilt carried, and the truth that could not yet be told.

The rain returned that evening, light and persistent, tapping the windows. Aaliya watched the droplets slide down the glass, feeling an unnamed comfort in the monotony, the constancy.

She did not know what had been left behind. She did not know what had been lost. But she felt, somehow, that the future — cold, unknown, and fragile — could be safe, too.

And in that fragile new home, the foundations of a slow, careful life began to take root.

Chapter 23

The afternoon sunlight slanted through the sheer curtains, painting the apartment in soft gold.

Khushi sat on the floor, a small doll clutched to her chest, eyes wide as she watched Aaliya move around the room.

"Hello," Aaliya said softly, kneeling to meet the child at eye level. Her voice was gentle, careful, a thread of warmth woven in despite the emptiness she felt.

Khushi tilted her head, a small frown of curiosity. Then, almost imperceptibly, she crawled forward, tiny hands reaching out.

Aaliya's chest tightened unexpectedly. She froze for a heartbeat — this instinct, this pull, felt ancient and unnamable. Something inside her stirred, though her mind could not place it.

"Khushi," Aaliya said, using the name with care, testing it on her lips. The child's eyes lit up.

"Ammi?" The word slipped out before Khushi could stop it.

Aaliya's breath caught. She blinked, heart hammering, unsure of what the word meant. Yet the tone, the weight, the meaning — it resonated somewhere deep within her.

"Ammi," Khushi repeated, climbing into her lap without hesitation. She pressed her small face against Aaliya's chest, arms wrapping instinctively around her.

Aaliya's hands trembled as they rested on Khushi's back. Her mind screamed — confusion, guilt, fear — yet the warmth of the child's trust, the certainty in her tiny arms, was undeniable.

"You... you're so small," Aaliya whispered, voice thick. "And yet... I feel like I've known you forever."

Khushi giggled softly, brushing her fingers through Aaliya's hair. "You're mine," she said simply, as if stating fact.

Aaliya's chest tightened, emotion threatening to spill over. "Mine..." she echoed. The word felt right, even if she did not understand why.

Ruhan watched from the doorway, silent, his chest tight. He had not expected this. The bond — instantaneous, instinctive, maternal — had emerged despite every lie he and Afsana had constructed. He clenched his fists, guilt slicing deeper than ever.

Afsana, standing slightly behind him, allowed herself a quiet smile. "The heart knows what the mind cannot yet remember," she murmured.

Aaliya rocked Khushi gently, whispering lullabies she didn't recall knowing. Her fingers stroked the child's hair, tracing the curve of her cheek. Every touch, every sound, reinforced a connection older than memory, deeper than explanation.

Khushi rested her small head against Aaliya's chest, eyes fluttering closed. "Stay," she murmured.

"I'm here," Aaliya whispered back, heart breaking and swelling at once. She had no right to feel this, no claim to this child — and yet, instinctively, she could not let go.

The afternoon drifted into evening, golden light fading to soft lamplight. Meals were shared, tea poured, stories whispered. Every movement was careful, protective, loving.

And in that quiet, ordinary intimacy, Aaliya felt a profound sense of belonging — a life she could touch but not yet fully know.

Jalebi the stray cat wandered into the room that evening, brushing against Aaliya's legs. She bent down instinctively to stroke him, the small orange cat purring against her palm, a soft anchor in the gentle chaos of new life.

Ruhan watched from across the room, the weight of the lie pressing heavily on him. He could see it — the mother in her, alive despite memory, alive despite loss. And yet, he knew the truth could never surface too soon.

For now, this fragile family, bound by care, instinct, and protective deception, breathed together in quiet harmony.

And somewhere in the golden lamplight, Aaliya began to understand — without words, without memory — that love could grow quietly, even in the absence of truth.

Chapter 24

The apartment was quiet in the early Delhi morning. Aaliya hummed softly while arranging breakfast, Khushi chattering beside her as she poured milk into a small cup.

Ruhan stood near the window, watching them from a distance. His hands rested on the sill, fingers twitching ever so slightly. He could have joined them. He could have laughed with them, shared tea, even smiled without restraint. But he didn't.

He couldn't.

Every glance at Aaliya, every small gesture of maternal instinct she displayed with Khushi, stabbed at him with guilt. Every instinctive touch she offered to the child — the child that was hers by right, not by story — reminded him of what had been lost, of what he had taken through recklessness, accident, and fate.

He moved quietly, unnoticed, setting plates on the table, filling cups with tea, arranging the breakfast tray with precision. No words. No smiles. Just service.

He lingered at the doorframe while Aaliya laughed at a story Khushi had told, her voice light, unburdened. A strange ache settled in his chest.

He wanted to hold her hand, to comfort her, to tell her everything. But that would destroy her — destroy the fragile threads holding her mind together.

And so he loved her in silence. Loved her through action, not confession.

When Khushi toddled toward him, carrying a half-eaten piece of toast, he smiled briefly, soft and unacknowledged. "Careful," he murmured. "Don't spill."

She nodded solemnly, then ran back to Aaliya. Ruhan's chest tightened. That simple exchange — small, ordinary — was enough to crush him with longing.

The cat, Jalebi, appeared at his feet, brushing against his legs. He bent down, stroking the soft orange fur, and for a moment, the weight on his shoulders eased. The cat purred, a reminder of life continuing, of comfort without question, of unconditional presence.

Ruhan straightened, returning to his silent observance. He cleaned, organized, tended — every task a prayer, every movement penance. Every act of care for Aaliya and Khushi was a way to atone, to serve, to exist without claiming what he could never have.

He felt every heartbeat of theirs as if it were his own. Every laugh, every breath, every small smile — reminders of what should have been his to protect fully, honestly, without deception.

He was their guardian. He was their provider. But he would never be allowed to be their equal in love, not yet, not ever — not until the truth could be faced.

And in that quiet, lonely vigil, he realized that survival and protection were not enough to calm the storm in his chest. Guilt, devotion, and desire coiled together, a relentless knot he could not untie.

Outside, Delhi's winter sun shone weakly through gray clouds. Inside, life continued, fragile, careful, and slow — a dance of love, loss, and secrets that no one dared speak aloud.

Ruhan would remain at the edge, loving silently, serving endlessly, and bearing the weight of what he had done.

And he would endure. Because she was alive. That was all that mattered.

Chapter 25

The Delhi winter seeped into the apartment, creeping under doors and around window panes, a subtle chill that nipped at fingertips and noses alike.

Aaliya moved around the kitchen in a soft sweater, hands wrapped around a steaming cup of chai. The aroma of cardamom and ginger filled the small space, curling around her senses like a gentle embrace. Khushi sat at the table, tiny fingers wrapped around her own mug, eyes bright, cheeks flushed from the warmth inside.

Ruhan stood a few steps away, hands tucked into the pockets of his coat. He watched quietly, careful not to disturb the scene, careful not to intrude on the moments that weren't his to claim.

"You made it perfect," Aaliya said softly, smiling at the steam rising from the cup. "Exactly how I like it."

Khushi laughed, a high, innocent sound that made something ache in Ruhan's chest. "Ammi!" she exclaimed, pointing at the frothy tea. "It's yummy!"

Aaliya reached over, brushing a strand of hair from Khushi's forehead. "Yes, it is," she said gently, unaware that the warmth she felt toward the child was more than habit — more than duty. She simply knew that the comfort and care she offered were necessary, natural, right.

Ruhan's throat tightened. He stepped closer, quietly placing a small plate of toast and jam on the table. "Breakfast is ready," he said softly, keeping his tone neutral, careful, watching for any sign of unease.

"Thank you," Aaliya said automatically, glancing at him, but the warmth of the smile was reserved for Khushi.

He nodded, accepting the distance he imposed on himself. Every smile she gave, every laugh she shared, belonged to her — not to him.

They ate in a rhythm of quiet intimacy, punctuated only by the occasional giggle or small comment from Khushi. The cold outside contrasted sharply with the warmth inside, and for a moment, the small apartment felt like a sanctuary, a fragile world apart from grief, guilt, and memory.

Afterward, Aaliya lingered at the table, sipping chai slowly. Her eyes followed Khushi as she scampered toward a small bookshelf. Ruhan stood silently, hands behind his back, watching over them, a silent guardian.

She didn't know why she felt a sudden pull — a gentle longing, a quiet flutter in her chest whenever Ruhan was near. She couldn't name it, couldn't place it, and so she ignored it. Yet the sensation remained, subtle and insistent.

Ruhan, feeling the weight of his own heart, focused instead on the mundane — refilling Khushi's mug, straightening a cushion, arranging the morning light as it fell on the floor. Every act of care was a penance, a devotion, a silent prayer.

And the cat — Jalebi — jumped onto the table quietly, settling beside Khushi. Aaliya bent to scratch behind his ears, his purr vibrating against her palm. The simple comfort of the cat, the child, and the warmth of tea created a fragile cocoon — one Ruhan maintained from the shadows, knowing every small happiness carried the weight of the truth he could not yet share.

Outside, Delhi streets were gray and cold. Inside, warmth, ritual, and quiet devotion blossomed slowly.

And though no one spoke of the past, or of the accident, or of the lives lost, the small domestic intimacy — chai, toast, laughter, and the soft purr of a cat — began to stitch the fragments of a new life together, thread by careful thread.

Ruhan's heart ached with every beat, but he stayed, loving silently, serving silently, protecting relentlessly.

Because she was alive. That was all that mattered.

Chapter 26

The streets of Delhi smelled of spice, smoke, and sizzling fried food. The winter air carried the tang of tamarind, fresh coriander, and the faint drizzle of leftover rain from the evening clouds.

Aaliya and Khushi walked ahead, bundled in scarves and coats, Khushi's tiny hand slipping into hers with instinctive trust. Ruhan followed a step behind, silent, observant, carrying the small purse of coins Aaliya had insisted he bring.

"Ammi, hurry!" Khushi giggled, tugging her mother toward a small stall adorned with garlands of bright chili peppers and strings of marigolds. "They have pani puri!"

Aaliya laughed softly, the sound catching in Ruhan's chest like a familiar ache. "All right, all right," she said, smiling at the crowd, at the smells, at the bright lights of the roadside stall. She felt a warmth in her chest she couldn't name — not yet knowing the truth of why it felt like home.

The vendor greeted them with a nod, deftly scooping crisp puris and filling them with tangy potato, chickpeas, and tamarind water. Khushi's eyes sparkled with anticipation as she watched the small, spicy morsels being prepared.

"Eat carefully," Aaliya said, handing one to her daughter. "Don't spill it all over your coat."

Khushi laughed, biting into the puri, juice spilling down her chin. Aaliya wiped it away with a napkin, smiling fondly.

Ruhan stepped closer, adjusting the scarf around his neck as he observed the scene. His hands itched to help, to reach out, but he stayed still, a silent observer of the warmth and laughter he could never claim.

"You're making me hungry too," he said softly, almost to himself, and Aaliya turned, smiling.

"Then eat," she said gently, pushing a puri toward him. "It's your turn."

He shook his head quickly. "No, you first. You two should enjoy."

Her eyes lingered on him for a moment, a fleeting spark of something unspoken — gratitude, curiosity, perhaps recognition of the quiet way he always ensured their comfort. Then she smiled at Khushi again and turned to take another bite herself.

The evening stretched around them like a soft shawl. Laughter, the crunch of puris, and the tangy zing of tamarind created a rhythm of domestic joy. And yet, under the surface, Ruhan felt every heartbeat, every breath, every small flicker of maternal instinct in Aaliya's actions, as if each moment reminded him of what had been lost — and what he could never confess.

Khushi leaned against Aaliya, cheeks flushed from the spice and the cold. "Ammi, you eat more!" she insisted, pressing another puri into her mother's hand.

Aaliya chuckled, accepting it with tenderness. "All right, little one," she said. "But I don't want to get a stomachache."

Ruhan watched the small tableau, heart tight. He was allowed to provide, allowed to observe, but not allowed to claim a single smile, a single laugh, a single touch that wasn't meant for her.

And as Jalebi the cat padded through the crowd, weaving between legs and sniffing the air curiously, a small, orange anchor in the chaos, Ruhan felt a strange comfort. Even here, in the middle of laughter, spice, and life, his penance continued.

Because he loved them — silently, invisibly, painfully — and that was all he could do.

The streets of Delhi glimmered with lamps and neon signs, the aroma of pani puri and fried spices mingling with winter air. Inside the warmth of shared moments, a slowburn intimacy blossomed, unspoken, unnoticed, but undeniable.

And though guilt shadowed every heartbeat, Ruhan allowed himself to savor the fleeting sweetness of the evening.

Because for now, she was alive. She was smiling. And that was enough.

Chapter 27

The winter sun dipped low, spilling golden light across the apartment, painting the walls in warmth that belied the chill outside.

Aaliya sat at the table, Khushi nestled in her lap, tracing letters in a notebook with careful concentration. Ruhan moved silently in the kitchen, washing dishes, the faint scent of cardamom chai lingering around him.

She watched him for a long moment, noting the curve of his shoulders, the deliberate care in his movements, the quiet attentiveness he poured into their daily life. Something inside her stirred — a feeling she could not name.

It was not the bond she felt with Khushi, which was instinctive, maternal, and undeniable. This was... different.

Her heart thumped in a strange rhythm, an unfamiliar warmth that spread from her chest to her fingertips whenever he smiled, even faintly, in acknowledgment of some small task done well.

"Ruhan," she said softly, voice barely above the hum of the radiator. "You... you always seem to know what to do."

He paused, hands submerged in soapy water, looking over his shoulder. "I... I try," he said quietly, brushing wet strands of hair from his forehead.

She nodded, suddenly aware of how close he was, how present he was in the small space of the kitchen, in the rhythm of the apartment, in the life they now shared. Her chest tightened in a way that felt both thrilling and terrifying.

She shook her head slightly, trying to banish the feeling. She was confused, guilty even, though she did not yet understand why. She had no memory of the past, no recollection of what they had lost, yet here was this pull — this warmth — stirring her heart.

Khushi clapped her hands suddenly, breaking the spell. "Ammi, look! I drew Jalebi!" She held up a small, orange scribble on a piece of paper.

Aaliya laughed softly, the sound light and bright. She ruffled Khushi's hair and then looked at Ruhan, who had watched the interaction silently. Their eyes met briefly, a quiet acknowledgment passing between them — a moment so ordinary, yet charged with something unspoken.

Her stomach fluttered, a sensation she hadn't known before. She shook her head, trying to ground herself. *It's just... care. She's alive. He's providing. That's all.*

But the feeling lingered, weaving itself into her chest, curling around her ribs like a secret warmth she could not explain, could not name.

Later, as she walked through the small living room, Ruhan handed Khushi a small snack, and she noticed the way his fingers brushed her hand — accidental, fleeting, yet electric in a way that made her pause.

Her heart skipped. She swallowed hard, eyes fixed on Khushi, trying to convince herself that it was nothing. Yet when she looked back at Ruhan, he was already looking away, silently bearing the weight of what could never yet be admitted.

That night, Aaliya lay awake, Khushi sleeping soundly beside her, Jalebi curled at the foot of the bed. She replayed the small moments of the day — the laughter, the shared glances, the fleeting touch — and a warmth unfurled inside her, confusing, tender, undeniable.

"I... I don't understand this," she whispered into the darkness, fingers brushing Jalebi's fur for comfort. "Why... why does it feel... like this?"

Her chest ached with the realization: she was beginning to fall. Slowly. Gently. Inevitably.

And she did not yet know how dangerous that feeling could be.

Ruhan, in the kitchen, cleaned quietly, unaware of the quiet gravity of the moment, unaware of how profoundly she had begun to notice him, feel him, need him — in ways words could not yet define.

And somewhere between tea, laughter, and evening shadows, the first fragile threads of love began to weave themselves into their lives.

Chapter 28

The first cold wind of Delhi winter swept through the slightly ajar balcony door, carrying with it the scent of rain-damp streets and faint spices from nearby vendors.

Ruhan had just returned from the market, hands full of vegetables and bread for the evening meal. As he set the bags down, a small movement at the edge of the balcony caught his eye.

A tiny orange cat, fur matted and damp, crouched behind the railing, eyes wide and luminous. It froze for a moment, then let out a soft, plaintive meow.

Ruhan knelt slowly, careful not to startle it. "Hey there... little one," he murmured. His voice, low and gentle, carried more instinct than intention, a quiet invitation.

The cat hesitated, then took a tentative step forward, nose twitching, ears alert. Ruhan held out a hand, and after a moment, it pressed its small head into his palm.

Jalebi. The name came to him unbidden, sweet and sticky like syrup. He whispered it, watching the cat's ears flick. The name seemed to suit the orange little creature perfectly.

Aaliya peeked into the kitchen, frowning at the unusual visitor. "Who's this?" she asked softly.

Ruhan straightened, brushing his hands on his coat. "A stray," he said simply. "Seems to have chosen us."

Khushi squealed from the table, pushing herself toward the balcony. "Can we keep it? Please, please?"

Aaliya smiled faintly, hesitant, but her gaze softened as she watched the tiny cat stretch, pawing playfully at Khushi's scarf. "All right," she said. "But only if it behaves."

Jalebi blinked up at Ruhan, tail curling around his leg. And in that quiet moment, he felt an unfamiliar lightness — a small comfort against the weight of guilt he carried daily. The cat needed him, in its small, instinctive way. And he... needed something that could ask for nothing but care.

For the first time since the accident, Ruhan allowed himself to breathe. The orange cat pressed against his ankles, purring softly. Every vibration was like a balm, a small, tangible warmth he could cling to.

As the evening unfolded, Khushi fed Jalebi tiny scraps of her dinner, giggling when he licked her fingers. Aaliya watched quietly, smiling faintly, unaware of the subtle shift in Ruhan.

He cleaned up the kitchen in silence, Jalebi following him step by step, and Ruhan realized that this small, seemingly inconsequential creature was more than a pet. He was a mirror of Ruhan's own need for care, for connection, for something steady in the storm of his guilt.

The cat leapt onto the couch, curling into a tight orange ball. Ruhan knelt beside it, stroking its fur with meticulous care. For the first time in months, he felt a small, private peace — a fragment of comfort that belonged entirely to him.

And though Aaliya did not yet know it, Jalebi's presence would slowly weave into the rhythm of their lives: a witness to laughter, sorrow, intimacy, and the quiet pull of feelings unspoken.

Outside, the city lights flickered, reflecting off wet streets. Inside, warmth, soft purrs, and gentle domesticity filled the apartment.

For Ruhan, the cat was more than a companion. He was a reminder that life — no matter how broken, how burdened with guilt — could still offer moments of pure, quiet solace.

And in the soft gaze of the small orange cat, Ruhan allowed himself to hope, even if only in secret.

Chapter 29

The apartment was quiet, bathed in the soft glow of a single lamp. Winter's chill pressed against the window panes, but inside, a fragile warmth lingered.

Ruhan sat on the edge of the sofa, shoulders slumped, eyes fixed on the floor. The day had been long — endless chores, small errands, careful oversight of Khushi and Aaliya. His chest ached with a familiar heaviness, a weight he carried alone.

A soft rustle beside his leg made him glance down. Jalebi, the small orange cat, had padded over, tail upright, eyes bright in the dim light.

"You're persistent," Ruhan murmured, a faint smile tugging at his lips. The cat mewed softly in reply, brushing its head against his ankle.

He let out a slow breath, curling a hand over the cat's back. The purr that vibrated through Jalebi was steady and insistent, a rhythm that seemed to echo the heartbeat Ruhan had almost forgotten he had permission to feel.

Night after night, Jalebi sought him out. The small creature would weave between his legs in the morning, follow him silently through the apartment, and curl beside him when he tried to steal a moment of rest.

Tonight, as he lowered himself onto the sofa, exhausted, Jalebi leapt up, curling against his side. The cat's warmth seeped into him, pressing gently against the hollow in his chest that grief and guilt had hollowed out.

"You... choose me, don't you?" he whispered, stroking Jalebi's soft fur. The cat purred louder, resting its head against his hand as though confirming it.

For the first time since the accident, Ruhan allowed himself to be still. No calculation. No penance. No careful distancing. Only the quiet, insistent comfort of a small, living presence that required nothing but care.

Aaliya's laughter from the kitchen, Khushi's small chatter about school and toys, the gentle hum of domestic life — all of it washed over him. And yet, it was Jalebi's presence that gave him permission to breathe, to exist without judgment, to be present without claiming what he could not yet admit he desired.

He leaned back, closing his eyes for a moment. The orange cat purred against him, and Ruhan felt a fragile thread of peace stitch itself into his chest.

It was a small thing, almost insignificant in the grand scale of guilt, loss, and the lies that tethered them together. But it was enough.

Enough to let him live. Enough to let him serve. Enough to remind him that even in the darkest hours, comfort could be found in the quietest corners — in a small, orange cat who had chosen him as much as he had chosen to care.

And as he drifted toward sleep, Jalebi curled tighter, tail wrapped protectively around his wrist, and Ruhan knew: he was not entirely alone.

For the first time in months, he allowed himself to hope that even silent devotion could carry a measure of solace.

Chapter 30

The apartment was quiet except for the soft rustle of newspapers and the faint purring of Jalebi, curled in Ruhan's lap. Afsana leaned against the kitchen doorway, arms folded, eyes sharp, reading the scene before her.

Aaliya laughed softly at something Khushi had said, her hand brushing against Ruhan's briefly as he helped the child with her jacket. The touch was fleeting, innocent, yet it did not escape Afsana's notice.

"Ruhan," Afsana called gently, though the weight behind her tone stopped him mid-motion. He looked up, aware immediately of the gravity in her gaze.

"Yes, Aunty?" His voice was careful, restrained.

She walked over, placing a hand lightly on his arm. "You care for them," she said softly, "I see it. You provide, you protect... but you must remember one thing."

Ruhan's chest tightened. He had anticipated this, yet the reminder stung sharper than expected. "Yes?" he asked quietly.

"You must not take what does not belong to you," she said firmly, her eyes meeting his. "Aaliya is fragile. Khushi... she is her daughter. Everything you do, every word, every gesture, must honor that. You are their guardian, yes, but nothing more — not yet, not until the truth can be faced."

He swallowed, nodding slowly. "I understand," he whispered. The words carried more than obedience — they carried guilt, restraint, and the quiet weight of devotion.

Afsana stepped back slightly, still watching him with careful scrutiny. "I know your heart is heavy. I know your penance has been long. But do not mistake love for permission. Respect her, always. Protect her, yes — but do not let desire blur the lines. Do you understand me?"

"I do," Ruhan said again, firmer this time. His gaze fell to Jalebi, the orange cat curled against his side, a tiny anchor in the sea of his restraint.

"Good," she said, softer now. "I trust you. But I will be watching. Always."

Aaliya wandered in then, oblivious to the tension, her laughter ringing like a fragile bell. She knelt beside Khushi, helping her adjust a scarf, and Ruhan's eyes followed her automatically, guilt tightening its grip.

Afsana watched him, silent but knowing. "You have your place, Ruhan," she said quietly. "Remember it. Protect them, but do not take from them what is not yours. Your heart... it must wait."

He nodded again, swallowing the ache that her words stirred in him. To protect was his duty. To love freely — even from a distance — was his penance.

And so he stayed, a quiet shadow at the edge of their lives, loving silently, serving faithfully, and obeying the line Afsana had drawn with gentle authority.

Outside, Delhi's winter wind rattled the windows. Inside, warmth, domesticity, and careful restraint held the fragile household together — a delicate dance of protection, love, and secrets too heavy to speak.

Ruhan knew the warning would stay with him, etched into his every gesture, every glance, every heartbeat. And he would honor it.

Because for now, their lives — hers, Khushi's, and even his own — depended on it.

Chapter 31

The afternoon sunlight filtered through the curtains, dust motes drifting lazily in the warm glow. Aaliya sat cross-legged on the floor, helping Khushi with a small jigsaw puzzle.

"Here, this piece goes here," Aaliya said softly, nudging a bright corner piece toward the child.

Khushi's small hand paused, eyes wide, and she leaned closer, pressing her little face against Aaliya's arm. "Ammi..." she whispered.

The single word struck like a lightning bolt. Aaliya froze, heart hammering. She felt the warmth in her chest twist, tighten, swell — a rush of instinctive love so deep and sudden that it nearly stole her breath.

"Khushi..." Aaliya whispered back, voice trembling. Her hands hovered uncertainly over the child, as if the word itself carried a truth her mind could not yet grasp.

Ruhan, standing a few steps away, stiffened. His chest tightened, and for a long moment, he simply watched, unable to move. Guilt clawed at him like fire. He had known this moment would come eventually, and yet, when it did, the force of it nearly shattered him.

Khushi giggled softly, unaware of the weight of her words. She pressed closer, snuggling against Aaliya's side. "Ammi," she repeated, this time with more certainty, as if stating a fact.

Aaliya's hands trembled as she stroked Khushi's hair, heart aching with a love she could not name, yet knew she could not deny. Tears threatened the corners of her eyes, unbidden and relentless. "I... I'm here, beta," she whispered, voice catching. "I'm here."

The room fell silent for a heartbeat, the only sounds the faint purring of Jalebi curled at Ruhan's feet and Khushi's small, steady breaths.

Ruhan's hands clenched at his sides. His chest ached with guilt, longing, and an unbearable knowledge of what he had done — the accident, the lies, the way he had tried to protect her while denying himself even the smallest comfort.

He stepped forward slowly, voice low, controlled. "It's... okay," he said quietly, though the words were meant more for himself than anyone else. "It's natural. Don't... worry."

Afsana, who had been quietly observing from the doorway, exhaled softly. Her eyes softened as she took in the scene: Aaliya's instinctive maternal response, Khushi's unwavering trust, and Ruhan's silent torment.

She stepped forward, voice gentle but firm. "Sometimes, the heart knows before the mind does," she said, placing a careful hand on Aaliya's shoulder. "It's alright, beta. It's alright to feel."

Aaliya nodded, swallowing hard, eyes still fixed on Khushi. The name — "Ammi" — hung in the air like a fragile promise, an undeniable pull toward something she could not yet fully understand.

Ruhan retreated to the edge of the room, shoulders heavy, watching the small scene of love and instinct unfold. He was a guardian, a provider, a shadow — but now, more than ever, the weight of his penance pressed down.

And yet, as he glanced at the soft orange curl of Jalebi beside him, he allowed himself a single, private thought:

Even amidst guilt, even amidst lies, love — in all its messy, uncontrollable forms — could not be contained.

For the first time, the unspoken truth pressed against him more insistently than ever. And he would endure, silently, because her heart, her life, her happiness — Khushi's instinctive trust — depended on him doing so.

The word lingered, unbroken and pure: *Ammi.*

And in that single utterance, a fragile thread of destiny began to tighten around all of them.

Chapter 32

The Delhi winter sun cast pale light across the living room, warming the soft rug where Khushi sprawled with her coloring books. Aaliya sat beside her, brushing stray strands of hair from the child's forehead, her touch gentle and instinctive.

Afsana watched quietly from the doorway, arms folded, eyes tracing the scene like a guardian surveying a fragile world.

For months, she had remained vigilant — wary of every glance, every gesture, every heartbeat that passed between Aaliya and Ruhan. She had known the danger in closeness, the weight of unspoken truths. And yet, here she saw something that softened even her wary heart: Aaliya's instinctive care, her tender patience, the undeniable glow of maternal love that could not be feigned.

Ruhan hovered a little distance away, organizing the small toys scattered across the rug. His movements were careful, deliberate — every act of service infused with devotion, yet restrained, always respectful of the boundaries Afsana had set.

Afsana felt the familiar pull of trust loosen its hold on caution. She had seen him in moments no one else had: soothing Khushi when she fell, quietly providing comfort, protecting her without claiming affection that did not yet belong to him.

Softly, she stepped closer, her voice quiet and deliberate. "Ruhan," she said. He turned, eyebrows lifting at the tone — a mixture of caution and warmth.

"Yes, Aunty?" he replied carefully, hands still occupied.

"I see how you care for her," she said, eyes flicking between Aaliya and Khushi. "And how you respect her... both of them. You are... patient. Steady. I will not pretend I trust blindly — not yet. But I see you, truly. And that counts for something."

Ruhan nodded, swallowing the lump in his throat. The words were simple, but they carried weight. Approval, recognition — permission to continue his silent penance with the faintest relief that his devotion was acknowledged, if only in private.

Aaliya looked up from Khushi, sensing the quiet exchange, though not understanding its full significance. She smiled faintly, a small warmth flickering in her chest at the rare softness in Afsana's gaze.

The child leaned against her, unconcerned with the subtleties of adult caution. "Ammi," Khushi murmured, and Aaliya's chest swelled. She stroked the child's hair, heart gentle, warm, and growing in ways she could not yet name.

Afsana exhaled softly, a small smile brushing her lips. She had feared the fragility of the mind, the danger of unspoken emotion, the risk of misplaced affection. And yet, witnessing this — witnessing life, laughter, instinctive love, and careful devotion — she allowed herself a moment of faith.

"Continue as you are," she said to Ruhan quietly, her gaze steady. "Protect them. Serve them. Respect them. And perhaps... someday, if the heart is true, all will find its way."

Ruhan bowed his head slightly, gratitude unspoken. The weight of guilt remained heavy, but in this quiet acknowledgment, he felt a small thread of hope — fragile, yes, but alive.

The room settled into soft harmony. Khushi's laughter, Aaliya's gentle hum, the faint purr of Jalebi at Ruhan's feet — a rhythm of domestic life, tentative yet steady, growing stronger day by day.

Afsana lingered a moment longer, then stepped back, her trust loosened just enough to let the slow burn of healing continue unimpeded.

And in that soft, golden light, Ruhan felt something he had not dared to hope for: the faintest permission to love quietly, without fear, without crossing the line... yet.

Chpter 33

The winter sun had long retreated, leaving the apartment bathed in soft lamplight. Shadows stretched across the walls, but inside, the room felt alive with quiet domesticity — the gentle murmur of Khushi reading aloud, Aaliya humming softly while folding laundry, Jalebi stretched across the windowsill, purring lazily.

Ruhan sat at the edge of the sofa, elbows on knees, hands clasped tightly. He watched them, heart constricting with a familiar ache.

Every small act of care, every laugh, every fleeting glance Aaliya gave — it stirred something he could not name, something forbidden and dangerous.

He could not let himself fall.

Because guilt ruled him with relentless precision.

Because he had taken too much already.

Because every smile she gave, every trust she extended, was built on a lie — a lie he had sworn to protect.

He reached for the tea cup on the table but paused mid-motion. Even this small, ordinary gesture carried weight. Every moment spent near her risked crossing a line he had no right to approach.

Aaliya called softly from the kitchen, "Ruhan, can you help Khushi with this puzzle?"

He rose, moving toward them, careful to keep his expression neutral. Every movement was deliberate, measured — never too close, never lingering too long. He could provide, he could protect, he could serve — but he could not take, could not claim, could not love openly.

As he crouched beside Khushi, adjusting a piece of the puzzle, he felt the heat of Aaliya's presence, the faint brush of her hand against his as she passed a pen. A sharp pang tore through him.

She glanced at him, a soft, unthinking smile playing on her lips. "Thank you," she said. Innocent, ordinary. And yet, it struck him like a chord — a reminder of what he desired but could never voice.

He straightened quickly, stepping back, brushing off the lingering tension. "It's nothing," he murmured, voice tight.

Alone later, he sat in the quiet of his room, Jalebi curled in his lap, purring softly. The cat's presence was a balm he did not deserve. Ruhan ran a hand through its fur, closed his eyes, and allowed himself a single confession to the shadows:

I love her. I have loved her since the first moment I saw her. And I cannot. I must not. I will not.

The words repeated in his mind, a mantra of self-denial. Every thought of touching her freely, of smiling without restraint, of claiming even a fraction of her warmth, was immediately countered by guilt, by memory, by the weight of the accident, by the lies that tethered their fragile household together.

Outside, the city murmured with life — distant traffic, occasional laughter, the faint hum of winter wind. Inside, Ruhan's heart remained a quiet battlefield: love and restraint, desire and penance, longing and fear intertwined in a relentless tangle.

He would endure. He had to.

Because she was alive. Because Khushi was alive. Because the truth could not yet bear the light.

And so he stayed — silent, watchful, devoted — loving without claim, caring without ownership, waiting for a day he could not yet see.

Chapter 34

The apartment felt unusually tight that evening, as if the walls themselves were pressing in with the weight of unspoken words. Khushi had gone to bed early, leaving only the soft hum of the radiator and the distant sounds of Delhi traffic to fill the room.

Aaliya sat at the edge of the sofa, arms crossed, eyes sharp. She had felt it for days — the way Ruhan lingered near her, the subtle intensity in his gaze, the small gestures that went beyond mere care. Something unspoken hovered between them, a tension that refused to be ignored.

"Ruhan," she said suddenly, voice firmer than she intended, "we need to talk."

He looked up from the pile of papers he was organizing, expression carefully neutral. "About what?" he asked quietly, though his chest tightened at the tone in her voice.

She leaned forward, hands gripping the edge of the sofa. "You know what. I can feel it. This... tension. Between us. Stop pretending it doesn't exist. I need you to be honest with me."

His jaw tightened. Every instinct screamed to protect, to shield, to remain silent — to keep her safe from truths that could shatter her. Yet, the look in her eyes, the weight behind her words, made him hesitate.

"Aaliya..." he began, voice low, measured. "There are things you don't... that you cannot know. And I cannot — I mustn't — speak of them yet."

Her eyes flared with a mixture of frustration and confusion. "You don't get to decide that, Ruhan. You think I don't notice the way you look at me? The way you hover? The way you... care?"

He ran a hand through his hair, closing his eyes briefly. "You don't understand," he said quietly. "If I speak, it could destroy everything. Everything you have left. Everything Khushi has. I... I cannot risk it."

"Risk it?" Her voice cracked slightly, emotion seeping through. "Ruhan, I'm not a child! I know there's something here. Something you're holding back. I deserve honesty!"

He opened his eyes, pain flickering in the depths. "And if I tell you... the truth could break you. And I cannot live with that. I cannot bear to see you hurt like that again."

She stood suddenly, frustration and desperation shining through her every movement. "You're already hurting me by hiding it! Every day, this... distance, this restraint... I can feel it. I feel it in every look, every touch you refuse to give. I can't pretend it's nothing!"

Ruhan's hands tightened into fists. He stepped closer, voice barely above a whisper. "I am protecting you. I am protecting Khushi. That is the only thing that matters. And if that means I must remain silent, if that means I must bear it alone, then so be it."

Aaliya's chest heaved. Her eyes filled with tears she refused to blink away. "I don't want secrets, Ruhan. I don't want silence. I... I need the truth. I need to know who you are, what you feel — even if it's hard, even if it's dangerous!"

The room seemed to hold its breath. The weight of their words, the history neither could fully name, pressed down, heavy and unyielding.

Ruhan looked at her, and for a fleeting second, his resolve wavered. The urge to reach out, to hold her, to confess everything, was nearly irresistible. But he clenched his jaw, forcing himself back into the role of protector, shadow, silent penance.

"I..." he started, voice breaking, "one day you will know everything. But not yet. Not now. I cannot risk it."

Aaliya's tears spilled freely now, and she sank onto the sofa, head in her hands. "I can't wait forever," she whispered.

Ruhan stepped back, chest heavy, and let her weep. Every heartbeat echoed with longing, regret, and the unbearable knowledge that love — his love — must remain silent, even as it burned brighter than ever.

Jalebi padded quietly to the sofa, curling against Aaliya's side as if sensing the storm in the room. Ruhan knelt beside the cat, silent, watching, feeling the weight of what he could not yet give, and knowing that the confrontation had only made the coming truth inevitable.

Because the moment to reveal everything — the accident, the lies, the child, the loss — was drawing near.

And neither of them could escape it forever.

Chapter 35

The wind bit sharply at the edges of the rooftop, tugging at scarves and loose strands of hair. Delhi stretched out below them, a sea of lights blurred by the winter haze.

Aaliya stood at the ledge, hands gripping the cold railing, eyes wide and resolute. Her chest rose and fell in rapid, controlled breaths. She did not intend to jump — not to die. But the danger of the edge forced attention, demanded truth, and left no space for evasion.

Ruhan stepped cautiously toward her, heart thudding violently. Every instinct screamed to pull her back, to hold her, to shield her. And yet, he knew that even his nearness could tip the fragile balance of control she held.

"Aaliya," he said carefully, voice low and steady, though every word carried the tremor of desperation. "Please... step back. Don't do this. It's dangerous."

She shook her head, eyes fierce. "I'm not afraid of danger, Ruhan. I'm afraid of lies. I'm afraid of not knowing. And I will not stand here pretending I don't feel it — whatever *it* is between us — while you hide everything from me!"

He took another step, careful to keep his tone calm, even as panic surged inside him. "I am protecting you. Protecting Khushi. You don't understand — if I tell you now, it could destroy everything. I cannot risk that."

Her voice rose, sharp as the wind. "I *can't wait*! I can't live in shadows and half-truths anymore! If you won't speak... then maybe you need me to face the edge to make you!"

Ruhan froze. His hands trembled. He could see the steel in her eyes, the absolute determination, the fearless pull toward the line. The very thought of losing her, even momentarily, even through a threat, tore through him.

"Aaliya!" His voice cracked, carrying the weight of months of guilt and restraint. "Do not! Please... don't do this! I cannot bear it if something happens to you. I swear to Allah, I will tell you everything — but not like this. Not yet. Step back!"

For a long moment, neither moved. Wind whipped around them, carrying distant car horns and the faint hum of the city. Ruhan's chest heaved. He knew that this edge — this moment — was a threshold. He could no longer hide behind silence without consequence.

Aaliya's eyes softened slightly, though they remained resolute. "Then speak. All of it. Now."

He swallowed hard, the weight of truth pressing down like the winter air itself. Every memory, every lie, every act of protection and guilt surged in his chest. The accident. Sonia. Zain. Khushi. The lie they had built together.

Ruhan closed the distance slowly, hands open, showing no threat. "Aaliya..." he began, voice trembling with the weight of confession. "Everything you need to know... I will tell you. But first, you must promise — whatever happens, you will not blame yourself, and you will not let this destroy you."

She nodded, determination mingling with fear. "I won't. Just... tell me everything."

He inhaled deeply, eyes locked on hers, heart hammering with every beat. "The accident... it was my fault. Sonia and Zain — they died. You survived. But the truth... Khushi — she is your daughter. Zain... he was your husband. Sonia was my closest friend."

The words hung between them, heavier than any winter wind.

Aaliya staggered back slightly, hand to her mouth. Her knees threatened to buckle, but she did not fall. She was trembling, a mixture of shock, grief, and something that felt like awakening.

Ruhan's chest ached, guilt and fear cutting through him like ice. "I lied to protect you. To let you heal. To keep you alive. I could not... I could not risk telling you the truth before now."

Aaliya's tears fell freely, the weight of the revelation crashing over her. Her eyes met his, searching, accusing, desperate, yet still flickering with the faintest trace of trust.

"I... I don't know if I can forgive you," she whispered, voice breaking. "I... I don't know if I can even believe you..."

Ruhan took a cautious step closer, hands trembling. "I am here. I will not leave. I will bear the pain, the blame... everything. But please, Aaliya... believe me when I say, I never stopped loving you. I never stopped protecting you. That is all I have left."

For a long, tense silence, the wind whipped around them. Jalebi's faint meow drifted from the apartment below, tiny and insignificant against the enormity of the moment, yet grounding.

Aaliya's chest heaved, mind spinning. The line between grief, rage, and something tender began to blur. She was standing at the edge — not just of the rooftop, but of understanding, of forgiveness, of the fragile start of something new.

And Ruhan, standing before her, silent and broken, waited for the choice she would make.

Because truth had finally arrived — and nothing would ever be the same again.

Chapter 36

The wind had calmed slightly, leaving a brittle silence on the rooftop. Aaliya's chest heaved with rapid breaths, eyes wide and unblinking, as if trying to contain the weight of what Ruhan had already begun to reveal.

He stepped closer, careful not to touch her, careful not to force her gaze, but every word he spoke carried the weight of months of hidden torment.

"I have to tell you everything," he said, voice low, trembling. "And you must hear it, even if it breaks you. Because you deserve the truth, no matter how painful."

Aaliya's lips parted, but no words came. She only nodded, heart hammering, hands gripping the railing.

Ruhan drew a deep breath. "The accident... it was my fault. Sonia — my closest friend — and I were driving that night. The rain made the roads slippery. I was careless, reckless even, drunk with... regret, anger, everything I couldn't face in myself. We collided with another car."

He paused, swallowing hard. The memory was sharp, jagged, a blade pressing into his chest. "The other car... it had you and Zain. They... they didn't survive."

Aaliya's eyes widened in horror. She stumbled back slightly, and he caught her gaze, forcing himself to continue.

"You did survive," he said quietly. "But your memory... everything you knew... it was gone. And I — I lied. I lied because I could not bear the thought of you remembering, of losing yourself all over again."

Tears began streaming down Aaliya's face. "I... I don't understand..." she whispered. "How... why?"

"Because," he said, his voice cracking, "you were fragile. Khushi — she is your daughter. Zain was your husband. Sonia was my closest friend. She... died that night. I... I could not tell you, so we created a story — a story to keep you alive, to let you heal, to let you live. I said... that Khushi was my daughter with Sonia. That you were her aunt. It was a lie. A terrible, unforgivable lie. And I have lived with it every day since, protecting you, serving you, loving you silently, while punishing myself for the pain I caused."

Aaliya staggered back, tears streaming, hands pressed to her mouth. The city below blurred into a haze of lights, inconsequential against the hurricane of revelation on the rooftop.

"You... you lied to me?" she whispered, voice barely audible. "All this time... everything..."

"Yes," he admitted, every syllable a wound. "I lied. I hid the truth to protect you from the grief you could not bear then. And I... I did it for you. Not for me. Every day, I have lived with the guilt. Every night, I have prayed for forgiveness. And every moment, I have loved you — without ever daring to speak it aloud."

The weight of it pressed down on her like the winter sky itself. Aaliya's legs shook. Her mind spun, memory and instinct colliding, grief and shock and confusion tumbling together.

"I... I don't know what to feel," she whispered. "I... I don't know if I can forgive you..."

Ruhan stepped slightly closer, his voice breaking, raw with emotion. "Then don't," he said gently. "Don't forgive me. Hate me if you must. Blame me. I will bear it all. I only ask — that you understand

I never stopped caring. I never stopped protecting. I never stopped loving. That is all I have left."

She sank to the ground, head bowed, trembling. Her hands gripped her knees as tears fell freely. She wanted to scream, to cry, to collapse, to run — to process a lifetime in a single moment.

Ruhan remained standing, silent, letting her absorb the truth. The rooftop wind tugged at his coat, brushing against his face like the sigh of the city itself. He had confessed everything. There was nothing left to hide.

Khushi's laughter, the faint purr of Jalebi somewhere below, the distant hum of Delhi life — it all felt impossibly distant, trivial, compared to the magnitude of what had just been revealed.

And yet, beneath the grief, beneath the anger, beneath the shock, something fragile began to emerge in Aaliya — understanding. Perhaps even mercy. Perhaps even love.

Ruhan's chest tightened, hope and fear tangled so tightly he could hardly breathe. He had offered her everything he could — truth, penance, and the most forbidden gift he had kept for months: his heart.

And now, all that remained was whether she would choose to take it — or let it remain broken, like him.

The wind stirred again, carrying the faint, comforting sound of a soft orange purr. Jalebi had found its place in this storm of truth, curled somewhere close, as if reminding them both: life, fragile and imperfect, could still carry warmth.

Aaliya lifted her head slowly, eyes wet, chest trembling. For the first time, she saw him fully — not as the man who lied, not as the man who caused pain, but as the man who had carried the weight of that pain for her, silently, faithfully, endlessly.

And in that moment, the slowest, most impossible chapter of their lives began to turn.

Chapter 37

The apartment was silent except for the faint rustle of curtains and the soft ticking of the wall clock. The city beyond the window blurred into indistinct shapes, distant car horns and winter wind reduced to background noise. Inside, a different storm raged.

Aaliya sat on the floor, knees drawn to her chest, tears streaming freely. She had heard everything — the accident, the lies, the truth of Khushi, Zain, and Sonia. Every word had struck her heart like a jagged blade.

Yet she could not remember. The past she had lost — her life before the accident — was a haze. Faces were shapes, names were sounds, memories were shadows. She grieved what she could not see, could not feel fully, could not reclaim.

Khushi approached slowly, small hands brushing against her mother's shoulder. "Ammi?" the child whispered, voice tentative, unsure.

Aaliya's chest tightened. She wanted to pull her close, to claim her as hers, yet a strange emptiness pressed against that instinct. She hugged Khushi anyway, feeling a pull she could not explain — a thread connecting them despite the absence of memory.

Ruhan stood a few steps away, silent, watching the scene with a heart torn between relief and agony. He wanted to reach out, to comfort her, to hold her, but he knew the fragility of this moment. She needed space to grieve. She needed to feel the weight of truth before any comfort could take root.

"I... I don't understand," Aaliya whispered into the quiet room, voice breaking. "Everything... it's too much. I... I'm not me... and I don't know who I am anymore."

Ruhan's chest ached. He wanted to tell her that she was still herself — that her instincts, her laughter, her care for Khushi, were the truest parts of her. But he only stayed silent, letting her feel what she must, bearing the weight of her grief in his own way.

Tears fell freely, soaking the sleeves of her sweater. Each sob was a small confession of loss — a life stolen, a husband gone, a child's past unknown, a friend lost forever. And through it all, the reality of what had been done, the accident, the lies, pressed down like a winter storm.

Khushi climbed into her lap, wrapping small arms around her neck. Aaliya buried her face in the child's hair, allowing herself a single, instinctive act of love. It was a thread — fragile, delicate, imperfect — but real.

Jalebi padded across the floor, rubbing against Ruhan's legs before leaping onto the windowsill. The orange cat purred softly, a small, grounding presence in the storm of grief. For Ruhan, it was a reminder that even in brokenness, small comforts could exist.

Hours passed in silence, broken only by tears, sobs, and the faint murmur of the city. Aaliya did not yet forgive, nor did she yet understand the fullness of her heart. She only grieved. She only felt the raw edges of reality pressing in, sharp and relentless.

And Ruhan stayed close, invisible but present, carrying her pain in the silence, holding the space between devastation and hope, knowing that the slow burn of healing had only just begun.

Because grief without memory was cruel and unrelenting — but it could not erase instinct, love, or the quiet, persistent bond between them.

And in that fragile space, Ruhan allowed himself to hope, even in the darkness, that one day she might forgive, might remember, might love again.

Chapter 38

The room was bathed in the soft glow of late afternoon sunlight, dust motes drifting lazily in the warm air. Khushi played quietly on the rug, absorbed in her coloring, while Jalebi napped curled on the sofa, tail flicking lazily. The ordinary rhythm of home hummed softly around them, fragile and precious.

Aaliya sat on the edge of the sofa, hands folded in her lap, eyes distant yet luminous. She had wept, raged, and grieved. She had felt betrayal, loss, and confusion. Yet beneath it all, a quiet voice — instinct, faith, something beyond reason — whispered to her heart.

Ruhan knelt a few feet away, silent, still carrying the weight of his confession, of his guilt, of every unspoken word left for months. He did not move closer; he did not speak. He waited, tense, for the judgment that could decide everything.

Finally, Aaliya lifted her gaze, eyes meeting his with a mixture of sorrow, understanding, and something like resolve.

"I..." she began, voice trembling, "I don't remember everything. I don't remember the past I lost, the life I lived, the people I loved. But..." She drew a slow, steadying breath, hands gripping the edge of the sofa. "...I see you. I see how you've carried everything for me. I see how you've protected me, loved me silently, sacrificed for me. And I... I forgive you."

Ruhan's chest tightened. His hands, resting on his knees, clenched slightly, unable to hide the tremor of relief and disbelief. "Forgive me?" he whispered, voice barely audible.

She nodded. "Yes. I choose mercy. Not because I understand fully, not because the past is clear, but because Allah guides hearts in ways we cannot always see. And I believe... this path, however painful, is meant to lead us somewhere. I forgive you — because to carry hatred would destroy me, and because to forgive is... the right thing to do."

Tears glimmered in her eyes, but this time they were tempered with grace, with acceptance, with a slow recognition of the strength in mercy.

Ruhan lowered himself to sit beside her, still careful not to touch without invitation, still reverent in his restraint. "Aaliya... I don't deserve your mercy. Not after everything. But I... I will spend every day proving that your forgiveness is not wasted."

Aaliya's hand hovered in the space between them, unspoken, uncertain. She did not yet fully remember, did not yet fully trust the past, but instinct and faith guided her. She let it rest, a silent acknowledgment that some things were beyond memory and reason, yet could still be true.

Khushi crawled into her lap, leaning against her chest. Aaliya hugged her tightly, instinctive love radiating through every small gesture. Jalebi stretched and purred, rubbing against Ruhan's arm, a quiet witness to the fragile reconciliation of hearts.

Ruhan exhaled slowly, allowing himself to stay, to exist in the fragile warmth of mercy, devotion, and hope. For the first time since the accident, he felt — not complete peace, but the possibility of it.

Because forgiveness had arrived. Slowly, quietly, irrevocably.

And the slow burn of healing — for all three of them — had begun.

Chapter 39

The morning sunlight was pale and diffused, spilling across the neatly packed bags lined by the door. Khushi tugged at Aaliya's sleeve, oblivious to the heaviness that hung in the air. Jalebi padded along the edge of the room, sniffing at suitcases, tail flicking nervously, sensing the quiet tension.

Aaliya stood, coat buttoned, scarf draped carefully around her neck. Her eyes were calm, almost serene, yet Ruhan could see the weight behind them — the mixture of fear, grief, and determination.

"I think it's time we go," she said softly, voice steady but not unkind. "Delhi... it has been good for us. But we need a fresh start. Afsana and I... we'll take Khushi home for a while."

Ruhan's chest tightened. He had known this moment might come, yet nothing could prepare him for the ache of possibility — that she might leave him behind. He forced his voice to remain calm. "If that is what you feel is right... then I will not stop you," he said quietly.

She met his eyes, a shadow of sadness crossing her face. "I know you've... given everything for us. And I know you will continue to. But we need space, Ruhan. For Khushi. For me. For... clarity."

He nodded, swallowing hard, though his heart screamed otherwise. "I understand. I only ask... be careful. And know... whatever you decide, whatever distance there is, my support will never falter. For both of you."

Khushi tugged at his sleeve, oblivious to the emotional storm. "Ruhan-uncle?" she said softly, eyes wide.

Ruhan bent down, brushing her hair back gently. "Always, Khushi. I'll always be here."

Aaliya watched, a faint smile ghosting across her lips, as she guided her daughter toward the door. Every step was deliberate, a test — a measure of the quiet restraint and devotion she knew Ruhan carried.

Jalebi meowed softly, rubbing against Ruhan's leg as if sensing the ache in his chest. He bent down to stroke the cat, hiding the tremor in his voice when he said, "Take care of them. Always."

Aaliya paused at the threshold, hand on the doorknob. She turned back, and for a heartbeat, the world shrank to the distance between them. "Ruhan..." she whispered. Her eyes held something unspoken — a question, a longing, a fragile thread that tied them together.

He swallowed, keeping his gaze steady. "Go," he said softly. "And remember... mercy and love can survive distance."

She nodded once, decisively, and stepped out, the door closing behind her with a soft click. Ruhan remained inside, heart heavy, hands gripping the edge of the table, Jalebi brushing against him for comfort.

The apartment felt emptier now, yet charged with unspoken possibilities. He knew the slow burn of healing, love, and destiny was far from over.

Because even in her absence, every thought, every heartbeat, every whispered prayer carried her nearer, even as she seemed farther than ever.

And he would wait. Patiently. Devotedly. Faithfully.

For love, after all, did not always demand presence. Sometimes, it demanded endurance.

Chapter 40

The Delhi winter morning was crisp, the sky pale blue with streaks of sunlight spilling over the quiet residential street. The apartment felt unusually alive — the faint scent of chai lingering in the kitchen, Khushi humming a tune as she arranged her toys, and Jalebi perched on the windowsill, tail flicking, alert to every movement.

Aaliya stood by the door, coat buttoned, scarf wrapped carefully, bag at her side. She had made her decision — to leave, to seek clarity and space. Yet her heart carried a quiet pull she could not explain.

Ruhan appeared in the hallway, voice calm but threaded with urgency. "Aaliya... wait."

She turned, surprised by the softness in his tone, yet sensing the gravity behind it.

"I cannot let you go," he said, taking a careful step closer. "Not because I cannot bear your absence — but because you deserve to choose, freely, knowing everything. You have carried so much — grief, confusion, fear. You deserve clarity, truth, and... love that is offered honestly."

Her hands trembled slightly, gripping her bag. "Ruhan..." she whispered, heart racing, the winter air suddenly too sharp, too heavy.

He knelt slightly, eyes steady, voice low and reverent. "I have loved you silently, protected you, and waited for the day you could see me — truly see me — without fear, without lies. That day is now. The choice is yours, Aaliya. No guilt, no obligation. Just... your heart."

Tears gathered in her eyes, and she felt a pull so deep, so inevitable, that she could no longer resist. Every instinct, every thread of her being, tugged her toward him. Slowly, carefully, she stepped closer.

"I choose you," she whispered, voice trembling, yet resolute. "Not because of the past, not because of guilt, not because anyone asks me to... but because I want to. Because my heart tells me this is right."

Ruhan exhaled, relief and joy flooding through him. He reached out gently, taking her hands in his, holding them as if they were fragile treasures. "Then I will spend every day proving that your choice was not wrong. That your trust, your mercy, your love — will never be wasted."

Afsana watched quietly from the doorway, a soft smile on her face, while Khushi clapped her small hands, beaming at the reunion. "Ammi... Ammi!" she exclaimed, wrapping her arms around Aaliya's waist.

Jalebi meowed from the windowsill, leaping lightly to Ruhan's shoulder before curling into his chest, purring like a quiet benediction over the room.

The nikah itself was simple, intimate — a quiet declaration before Allah, in the modest living room that had witnessed months of grief, love, and healing. No grandeur, no spectacle, only intention, devotion, and destiny woven into every whispered vow.

Ruhan and Aaliya recited their words softly, deliberately, the air between them charged with tenderness, faith, and the quiet knowledge that they had survived everything to arrive here.

Khushi leaned against them, a warm bundle of instinctive trust, while Afsana placed a gentle hand on Aaliya's shoulder, eyes glimmering with approval and relief. Jalebi purred in the corner, tail flicking, the silent witness to a home restored.

As the final words were spoken, a sense of calm settled over the apartment. The past — grief, lies, and loss — had not been erased, but it had been acknowledged, forgiven, and transformed.

And in that quiet domestic intimacy, with the city below them continuing its hum, Ruhan and Aaliya found a love both inevitable and fragile, enduring and sacred.

Because destiny, like faith, moves in quiet, patient ways — and sometimes, it arrives exactly when it is meant to.

And so, the household — human and feline alike — settled into a rhythm of warmth, mercy, and devotion, hearts entwined, slowly, fully, finally home.

Jalebi curled at their feet, purring, a small orange flame of witness to love that had waited its entire life to burn.

www.ingramcontent.com/pod-product-compliance
Lightning Source LLC
LaVergne TN
LVHW022052200926
848481LV00003B/872
9798232974763